FREDDIE vs. THE FAMILY CURSE

FRED FAMILY

WITHDRAWN

DIE VS. THE CURSE

BY TRACY BADUA

CLARION BOOKS

AN IMPRINT OF HARPERCOLLINSPUBLISHERS

BOSTON NEW YORK

Clarion Books is an imprint of HarperCollins Publishers.

Freddie vs. The Family Curse

Copyright © 2022 by Tracy Badua

ISBN 978-0-35-861289-6

Typography by Celeste Knudsen
22 23 24 25 26 PC/LSCC 10 9 8 7 6 5 4 3 2 1

First Edition

For Ruby and Rahul

ONE

*T*HERE'S NOTHING MORE HEART-STOPPING THAN THE
wheeze of an empty glue bottle the night before a big
school project is due.

"Come on come on come on." I shake the bottle and
squeeze again. Not one white glob of grade-saving adhesive.
Not even a drop.

I chuck the bottle toward my trash can. It sails clear over
the heap of school uniforms on my bed, past an ankle-high
stack of old notebooks and worksheets.

I miss.

I thump my forehead down on my desk and sigh. My
eyebrow lands in a wet smudge of green paint.

The curse. Got to be the curse. Like straight black hair
and those little chicken-skin bumps on my upper arms, bad
luck is in my genes.

I guess I should be thankful that at least my whole family tree board hasn't spontaneously combusted. I transfer my precious deck of Robo-Warrior cards over to my bookcase, just in case. My cards will stay nice and safe next to my geography bee participation trophy and the palm-size Virgin Mary figurine from Grandpa Carlo.

Bad-luck curse or not, I need to finish this board to have any hope of keeping those Robo-Warrior cards. Mom threatened to take away the deck if my social studies grade slips any further. After a worksheet fluttered down a storm drain and a report jammed our printer so badly we had to scrap the whole machine, I can't afford another missed assignment. That Robo-Warrior deck is the only thing standing between me and total lunchtime isolation: the only thing that makes the other seventh-graders forget years' worth of my clumsiness and mishaps. I lean back and peer over at my cousin's open, lit-up window.

We live in an older and more crowded part of the suburbs, and the distance between my window and Sharkey's is exactly ten feet. If anyone would have glue, it'd be my perfect-at-everything cousin.

I slide open my window. Music blares from the top-of-the-line tablet Sharkey gets to use when she's done with homework, a reward for her straight A pluses last year. Meanwhile, my parents' strict restrictions on screens, phones, tablets, and any digital connection to the outside world basically push me back into the Stone Age. The only reason I even have a cell phone is so they can tell me when they'll be late to pick me up after school. And that cell phone is now locked and docked in the kitchen, off-limits the second we get home.

I yell to my cousin across this small divide.

"Hey, Sharkey, you there?"

I don't see her, but her voice sails between our houses. "Leave me alone, Freddie. *America's Dance Champs* is streaming live."

"It's an emergency!"

There's a frustrated groan and the squeak of a chair before Sharkey appears at her window. She's holding Auntie Sisi's Pomeranian, Biscuit. They both glare at me for the interruption. Sharkey's already in her pajamas: a faded Yellowstone National Park T-shirt from our family vacation two years ago (during which I stepped in bison dung) and purple bike shorts. "You have ten seconds."

"You got any glue?"

She shakes her head, and her shiny, black, chin-length hair swishes around her round, light-brown face. There was a brief time, as preschoolers, that she and I had the same bowl-shaped haircut. I don't know if that old haircut is better or worse than the one I sport these days.

"Sorry. Fresh out. Used the last of it on my board yesterday." She tosses in a satisfied smirk, rubbing a handful of verbal salt into my wounds. She's the one who suggested I start my project earlier, but I spent the last few afternoons lost in a paperback Robo-Warrior strategy guide.

I groan and loll my head back.

"Maybe your dad has some in the garage. He has everything in there," she adds. She's trying to be helpful, but the thought of digging around my family's overstuffed, cobwebby cavern of a garage grosses me out. She begins to shut the window. "Good luck with your project."

Her voice and the tinny pop music behind her fade away.

The whole house trembles with the rumble of thunder. San Diego isn't known for its April showers, but now sheets of rain start to smack against the roof.

I barely close my own window in time to keep the carpet from getting soaked. My shirt looks like I tried to drink a glass of water and missed my mouth completely.

I trudge toward the kitchen. My eyes rove the cluttered house for anything I could use to paste together this thick poster-size board, the handwritten name and date plates, and all those leaves I had to cut out for the "tree" visual. But dusty wineglasses, fake orchids, and a faded reprint of da Vinci's *The Last Supper* aren't going to help me demonstrate my A-plus-worthy (okay, B plus, if we're being honest) knowledge of my family tree.

Mom sets down her tea when my bare feet slap onto the cold kitchen linoleum. Her long black hair is pulled back into a ponytail, and she's got her purple-rimmed reading glasses on as she sorts the pile of mail in front of her.

There's even more mail stacked on the speckled gray countertop. A few weeks' worth of ads and bills are wedged between the coffee maker and the microwave that's been unplugged for months. What's that saying? Mail, mail, everywhere, but not a drop of glue?

Mom frowns at the speck of paint on my brow. "How's the project, Freddie? Almost done?"

I shift from side to side. No point in fudging the truth about my procrastination. She'll find out anyway if I get a bad grade back on my progress report.

"Almost. Ninety-nine percent of the way there. But I'm out of glue."

I wince at the I've-told-you-time-and-time-again look that flares in her dark brown eyes. My eyes are like hers, though mine probably look a lot more nervous.

"Can you use a stapler?" Her annoyance drips out with every word. Her mouth is a leaky faucet of disappointment.

I shake my head. "All out of staples. I used the last ones

on my book report last week." I'd spent an hour fishing misshapen staples out of the faulty hunk of metal. The Ruiz family curse isn't the darkest, most dangerous one ever cast, but it sure makes my life a lot trickier.

As if seventh grade isn't tricky enough.

"How about rice?" Mom asks.

I shudder at the memories of projects cobbled together with last-minute rice substitution. I should've learned my lesson about keeping a full bottle of glue on hand after that lumpy *White Fang* collage last year. But I'd rather take smeared sticky rice over the current alternative: a stick-figure tree and a handful of loose paper leaves.

If I don't find some adhesive soon, I might as well hand over my Robo-Warrior deck to Mom now and plan on eating lunch alone this week.

"Do we have any rice left?"

Mom lifts her teacup and takes a sip. "Look with your eyes, not with your mouth, Freddie."

I peer into the rice cooker, in its permanent place of honor next to the free calendar we got from the Asian supermarket. The metallic gray pot is missing.

"What's with the cereal on the floor?" I ask, edging past the crunchy mound of sugary Os to cross the kitchen.

Mom shrugs. "Your dad wanted something sweet after dinner and spilled. But we can't clean it up until morning.

You know what Apong Rosing would say if she caught us sweeping at night."

"Sweeping out the fortune," I say, repeating the warning drilled into us by Dad's superstitious grandmother. I leap over some already crushed Os to reach the sink.

My heart dives when I find the rice pot soaking, empty. We usually cook enough rice to feed an army, but Apong Rosing must have had an appetite tonight, of all nights. She tends to be hungrier on days when she has dialysis, a treatment that cleans her blood because her kidneys need a little help doing so. And none of us are ever going to deny our tiny but fierce elder a second or third serving.

"Nothing left. Can't we just go buy glue? It'll be quick, I promise."

A fresh clap of thunder rattles the sliding glass door. "No way we're going out in this weather, Freddie. Other people don't know how to drive in the rain." She sets down her teacup. "Besides, do you know how expensive gas is?"

"Yes, Mom." Because Dad grumbled about it when we got stuck in traffic on the way home today. "I guess I'll check the garage, then."

Mom nods. "Good idea."

Of course she likes Sharkey's solution and not mine.

I sweep a weak beam of light around the dark garage, squinting as I make my way to the toolbox. The flashlight's flickering glow skims piles of chipped-paint folding chairs, frayed cardboard boxes, and probably a dozen spiders waiting to pounce on me. The batteries in this flashlight are dying, and the garage lightbulb is broken.

Apong Rosing first told me about the Ruiz family curse when I was nine. Sharkey and I, surrounded by our hard-earned trick-or-treat stash on the living room carpet, tore into our favorites. Two bites into an Almond Joy, I started coughing when a piece of coconut stuck to my windpipe. Apong dislodged it with a hearty slap on my back. Screeching, Mom insisted that she either cut up my Halloween candy into sensible bites (like they do for toddlers) or that I give up the whole bag. When I complained, Apong sided with me.

"It's not Freddie's fault," Apong had said, stealing a Reese's from my pile on the floor. "These annoyances are all part of the family curse."

At first, I hadn't believed her. Sharkey and I had even laughed at the idea that bad luck had haunted my dad's family across generations. Dad and Mom declared it all pure nonsense. Mom monitored me as I meticulously chewed through one fun-size bag of M&M's, then she brought the rest of my candy to work the next day.

But after suffering through a scientifically higher-than-normal amount of bad-stuff incidents—stumbles off the school stage, randomized cafeteria cleanup jobs that always pin me with the grossest tasks, and worst of all, ending up the target of not one, but two bird poops on picture day—I had to admit the truth.

I'm cursed.

Bad luck follows me like toilet paper stuck to my shoe.

Want to try a new activity? Dive into something you enjoy? Most kids don't give these things a second thought. I know Sharkey doesn't. She climbs up and up, with her stellar grades and growing hordes of close friends. She and most kids don't have to worry about some curse randomly tripping them up and making them look foolish in front of the entire school. They don't have to play it ultrasafe just to get through the day without giving anyone a reason to point and laugh and whisper. But then again, she and most kids aren't cursed.

No glue in the toolbox. Only some mismatched nuts, screws, and nails. I shove the whole thing aside. If I continue rooting around in there, I'll probably end up pricking myself with a rusty screw and getting tetanus.

I wriggle past a stack of plastic bins marked CHRISTMAS to reach the worktable. I grab the handle of the top drawer, as rusty as the nails and screws I just sifted through. My palms are damp from the moisture in the air. I tug once: not even a budge.

Tightening my hold on the drawer handle, I pull again. This time, the drawer creaks open a half inch. I shift the flashlight to my other hand, plant my feet, and yank.

The drawer flies out of the table. I stumble back, landing on a lumpy garbage bag of clothes that should've been donated months ago. The drawer's contents clatter across the floor.

I inspect all the junk strewn around me. My flashlight beam lands on a small tube with a red cap partially hidden underneath some yellowed receipts and rusty safety pins. I reach for the tube and prick my finger on an open pin.

Holding my breath, I twist open the red cap. A drop of clear glue shines in the light. My shoulders droop in relief just as the storm lets out another boom of thunder. I screw the tube closed quickly, preserving every possible dot of glue.

As I shift to stand, a gleam of gold on the floor twinkles in the flashlight's bluish beam. It must have been tucked away in the drawer with the glue. I reach out carefully. My fingers brush a piece of metal, warmer than it should be in this stormy weather.

I scoop it up and inspect it. It's a thick gold coin dangling from a dirty, cracked string of leather. The gold buzzes, almost electric against my skin.

Lightning flashes through the side-door window, casting light on the coin's faint features. There's an outline of what must have been a face. Whatever nose, eyes, and mouth had been cast into this thing have long since worn away. Around the face are long vertical pillars, like prison bars. There must have been words surrounding the sun on the other side of the coin, but those are unreadable now too.

The flashlight dies, and I sigh into the darkness.

I stumble my way out. When I shut the door behind me, an odd shiver slithers down my spine, as if someone—or *something*—followed me out of the garage. There's no one else in the hallway, though. Must be the damp from the storm.

Shoving away the icky feeling in my gut, I pocket the superglue and coin.

I've got a family tree to save.

TWO

YAWN WIDE.

It's Tuesday, which means morning Mass day at Holy Redeemer Academy. All of us seventh-graders are up near the top of the creaky wooden bleachers, wedged between the eighth-graders above and the lower grades below. Despite her usual attempts to stay as far away as possible from you're-so-klutzy-and-embarrassing me, Sharkey's on my right. There are hundreds of us in the same blue and white uniforms, so if I fall asleep, the teachers won't be able to pick me out of a crowd, right?

I shake the daring thought out of my head and pray some of the sleepiness goes with it too. With my terrible luck, I'll probably plunk straight out of the bleachers and land at Father Walter's loafered feet.

It takes a kick to the shin from Sharkey for me to realize that the rest of the school is standing.

"Keep up!" she whispers.

Easy for her to say. She didn't stay up all night, hunched over construction paper pieces and superglue.

The Ruiz family curse only affects Ruizes, and she's a Mendoza. Her father is my mom's second cousin, or something like that. I'm honestly not a hundred percent sure, because Mom and Dad make me call every other Filipino we know uncle, auntie, or cousin.

I scramble to my feet and raise my palms to the sky like everyone else is, waiting for Father Walter's cue to start the prayer.

From the waist up, Sharkey is a model Holy Redeemer student. But, as usual, her sneakers tap to a beat playing in her head. She's one of the star b-girls on the Wyld Beasts, the best youth break-dancing crew in the county. With their Spring Showcase coming up, she takes every free second to run through her dance moves, physically or in her head. From the looks of some of the other fidgeting feet around me, a couple of her crew members in our class—messy-curled Dale, who thinks he's too cool to be friendly, and freckled Layla, always in a sweater two sizes too big—are doing the same.

Part of me wishes I could hear and move to that beat like Sharkey does. But complicated moves, inherited clumsiness, and bad luck don't mix, and I've found that runs true in most of the activities the other seventh-graders love. My lifelong streak of bad luck even got me kicked out of orchestra, when a wide swing of my trumpet case sent all the music stands toppling over like dominos. Sometimes, being cursed is more lonely than I'd like to admit.

I shuffle to my right to avoid getting kicked in one of Sharkey's stray moves, and something thunks lightly against my leg: the amulet.

My fingers itch to bring it out for a better look.

I was analyzing it at breakfast this morning when Apong Rosing spotted it. She said it belonged to her brother, Ramon.

"It's an anting-anting. An amulet, or a kind of good luck charm that keeps the owner safe from harm. Some people even believe anting-anting give them . . ." She flitted her wrinkled brown hand in the air, like she was drawing the correct English word out from the cosmos. "Magical powers. Different people will tell you different rules about anting-anting, but no one doubts magic this powerful."

Her mention of luck had made me curious. An anting-anting that could bring good luck—or heck, even nonbad luck—would be life-changing. I've got a list a mile long of things I want to try, or try again, without the worry of getting hurt, embarrassed, or (and most likely) both. Dance crews, band, any other group activity requiring coordinated, nonclumsy movement: this coin might be the key to all of it.

But then Apong went on to talk about reviving this old anting-anting with an albularyo or a priest. At the notion of activating jewelry to unlock magic, Dad handed me my lunch and shuffled me off to school.

Then he gave me the routine warning against believing my great-grandmother's Filipino fairy tales and not encouraging her "nonsense." He and Mom were both born here, and Dad says he had a hard enough time fitting in without the added layers of superstition and beliefs from overseas. So my parents' solution is to reject all of it, despite what Apong and I think, and they don't even want to hear a word otherwise.

Don't get me wrong: my parents love and value Apong, but balancing this respect for her and their heritage with what they think "American" looks like is an everyday struggle. Which is why I can't speak any Filipino languages but Dad still waited until morning to sweep up his cereal mess.

I can't shake the feeling that there's something to Apong's tale about anting-anting that holds just the smallest ounce of truth. Or maybe it's just me really hoping it's true, because of how much I need that good luck.

No matter how much I want to take a second look at the

coin, the teachers' eyes scan the bleachers like prison spot-lights, so I decide against it. I keep my hands lifted and start the prayer with everyone else.

"Our Father . . ."

I stop. The words that flow out of my mouth don't sound like my own.

I clear my throat with a quick cough and join the prayer again. Still, something sounds weird. My words come out with an eerie echo, like there's a chorus of a dozen voices whispering along with me.

Is this a prank?

A shadow flits at the edge of my vision. I glance around, expecting to catch some of the other seventh-graders gig-gling at me, but no one's paying me any attention.

Creeped out, I stop speaking altogether. To my horror, these faceless whispers go on without me, now joined by the low beat of faint drums.

I can't figure out where the drums are coming from. They're definitely not coming from Ms. McCoy's decade-old keyboard.

A warm breeze brushes my neck, despite the solidly closed gym doors. The air grows humid and smells of lush plants and damp earth. There's no way those scents could've come from outside: there's only blacktop and mud surround-ing the building.

My pulse picks up. I struggle to make sense of what's happening, all without drawing the attention of my hawk-eyed teachers. Sure, I had a late night finishing up the family tree board, but the lack of sleep wouldn't explain these hallucinations. Is this food poisoning? How old were those eggs that Dad cooked this morning?

A growing heat at my side snags my thoughts away from breakfast. I peer down, trying to pin the source. All the spit in my mouth evaporates when I notice the glowing golden circle in the pocket of my navy blue pants.

The amulet.

I lower one of my hands to fish the coin out. I have no desire to test the flammability of these uniforms.

From the side of the bleachers, one of the teachers gives a pointed cough. I glance up in time to see her raise her eyebrow at me.

Smoldering pants or detention and the wrath of my parents? I gulp and make a quick decision. I force my hand back up to prayer position and manage to join the rest of the school for the final "Amen."

With the prayer over, my senses slowly right themselves. I blink, and the shadows that had crept at the corners of my eyes disappear. The stale air of the gym has returned. My ears no longer ring with phantom voices or unseen drums. The amulet in my pocket has cooled and stopped glowing.

But, arguably worse, I'm the only one still standing. Sharkey, lips pressed tight in a frown, tugs at my belt loop to pull me down to my seat.

Giggles flutter out from the eighth-graders behind me somewhere, and my face warms. I drop onto the bleacher with a thud.

Sharkey leans over, her choppy black bangs swinging across her forehead. On her face is the teensiest hint of worry —just enough to outweigh her annoyance with me. "What's wrong?"

With the teachers' eyes back on Father Walter, I pull the amulet out of my pocket. Where there had been a vague outline of a person on the coin's face this morning, there's now the beginnings of eyes, a broad nose, a full mouth, and a sharp chin. I blink hard, but the evidence stares back at me: the solid gold amulet is somehow restoring itself. A chill shoots all the way down to my toes.

I peek up at Sharkey, and I'm surprised I'm able to form words to answer her question at all. "Everything."

THREE

I SLAM THE BATHROOM STALL SHUT AND PRESS MY BACK against the cold metal. My heart has kept up its unhealthy galloping since the second I noticed the change in the amulet. My class has PE right after Tuesday Mass, so I only had to stumble a few feet toward the boys' locker room after Father Walter dismissed us. This gives me a good five minutes to clear my head and change into my PE clothes.

My fingers trembling, I remove the amulet from my pocket. I squint to inspect it, hoping that what I saw earlier was just a trick of the bluish gym light.

But no, I see it even clearer in here. There is definitely a face where just a worn outline used to be.

"What is going on?" I whisper to myself. I run my thumb over the coin, confirming that it's still made of the same solid gold.

Then the eyes in the coin face blink.

My screech echoes through the entire bathroom. The amulet slips out of my hands, and I barely catch it by the leather string before it plops into the toilet.

The main bathroom door creaks open with some of the boys in my class heading for the locker room. Dale's bragging about going ATV riding this weekend, and another boy, Benjamin, is asking someone to sniff his PE shirt to see if it's clean.

I stifle my loud breathing. I don't want to draw any more attention to myself after my awkwardness during Mass. They already think I'm weird. And if I want to avoid the wrath of the PE teacher, Mrs. Barnes, I need to get out of this bathroom stall and get changed too.

But no way am I going to run laps around the track with an eye-blinking gold coin in my shorts pocket. I start to shove it into my bag.

"Hoy!" a faint voice calls.

Oh no.

My mouth goes desert dry.

I don't think I want to know where that voice is coming from.

Maybe I plummeted off the bleachers and am hallucinating all of this while EMTs are desperately trying to bring me back to consciousness. At least then I'd have a reason for seeing and hearing these things that make zero sense.

Summoning all my courage, I lift the coin up to my eye level.

The face of a teenage boy, now clear cut on the coin, frowns. "Who are you?" it snaps.

"Freddie. Who are you?"

No big deal. Just talking to a coin in the bathroom.

The boy purses his lips, like he doesn't want to answer. How does a phantom coin face have so much attitude?

"Ramon. Ramon Ruiz," he says after a moment.

My legs almost give out beneath me. Ramon Ruiz.

I know that name.

From the fog of my thoughts comes the realization that I recognize his face too. It's that smug seventeen-year-old in the yellowing, fake-mother-of-pearl frame on Apong Rosing's oak dresser. It's a portrait of her family: her father, dapper in a suit; her mother, glamorous in a long Maria Clara gown. A six-year-old Apong Rosing—simply Rosa back then—stares impishly into the camera. Her brother, already as tall as their father, stands straight-backed next to her with his sharp chin held high. They were wealthy and happy then. But that was before World War II crept onto the shores of the Philippines. Filipinos and Americans fought against the invading forces of Imperial Japan. Apong and her parents fled into the mountains for safety. But her brother didn't join them.

And I'm staring at him right now.

"You're Apong Rosing's brother," I mutter. "I'm—you're my—I'm your great-grandnephew." I'm torn between excitement and sheer panic. "How is this possible?"

Ramon barks out a laugh. "How is what possible? That I've been trapped in this anting-anting for ages? Or that I'm talking to you?"

I splay my hand against the stall wall, trying to steady myself. Ramon had voiced only a couple of the million questions buzzing around in my brain.

It's seeming more and more likely that I plummeted off those bleachers. I pinch my arm hard and yelp at the pain. Nope, I'm still alive and awake. This is really happening somehow. I gawk at the coin. Ramon gawks back.

"What did you do to this anting-anting?" he asks, his eyebrows furrowed. He looks just as confused as I feel. "Why is it that I can see and talk to you? I could not do this with anyone before."

His eyes narrow at me, like I've done something wrong. It's the same look Apong Rosing gives me all the time.

"I didn't do anything!" I snap. "I found this amulet and brought it to school, and then during Mass, I—"

The realization snatches the words out of my mouth. Apong Rosing had said something about priests or albularyos turning anting-anting on. I must have done it myself during chapel, by joining in Father Walter's prayer. My heart leaps. She said these bring good luck and protection, both things a cursed kid like me desperately needs. This anting-anting could be my key to success (or, more likely, middle grade mediocrity, which sounds just as good).

"I've awoken the anting-anting," I whisper almost reverently. My mind races to all the normal seventh-grade things that I can finally do, armed with this good luck charm: play games at the school carnival, learn some inline-skating tricks, actually speak up in a group project!

Ramon's eyes widen. "Stand back. I am going to try to finally leave this prison."

I've locked myself in a tiny bathroom stall. I've got nowhere to go.

Ramon shuts his eyes tight, and the whole coin starts to glow a warm, eerie green.

My excitement takes a backseat as my stomach sinks, then takes a total splat onto the floor when I see what Ramon's done.

Some sort of life-size ghost version of him floats in front of me. He wears a khaki-colored military uniform that's fitted on top and baggy around the legs, and he has a circular metal helmet tucked under his arm. He's see-through, and he's technically standing where the toilet is. His skinny legs move around it like it's not even there. Or like *he's* not even there.

I think I'm going to pass out.

His shoulders slump in disappointment. "It appears I'm still bound to the anting-anting. I thought perhaps you had broken the curse so that my spirit could move on, but I should've known. You are no hero. You are just a short boy with a wrinkly shirt and an odd haircut."

I scrunch my face at his offhand insult. I should be offended, but it's more important that I get answers than snap back at this rude ghost. "So you're affected by the Ruiz family curse, too, then?"

"Yes, it's how I ended up in here." He gives a long sigh, but then something lights up his face. "But you! Now that I can actually speak with someone, you will help me break this!"

A bang on the bathroom doors makes both of us jump.

"Two minutes, boys!" Mrs. Barnes hollers.

Finding a good luck charm that will not only counteract a curse but somehow break it? It's more than I'd hoped for when Apong first explained anting-anting this morning. I'll be a hero to the whole Ruiz family if I pull this off, whether Dad and Mom recognize the curse or not. But I guess the citizens of Metropolis don't recognize every time Superman saves them from certain destruction.

For a second, I consider how much trouble I'll be in if I hide in the bathroom stall the rest of the day, prying more of the story out of my great-granduncle. But my parents are already annoyed by my last-minute-project crisis, and ditching class is not an option. Mom would confiscate my Robo-Warrior cards and this amulet for weeks. Plus I'd be the laughingstock of the school if I was caught having a conversation with a coin. Next to the toilet.

I look Ramon right in his semitransparent eyes. "Count me in! I need you to tell me all about breaking this family curse, but first I have to go change into my PE clothes. We'll finish this later, okay?"

Ramon nods in understanding, but then a worried look sweeps over his face. "One last thing: stay alert." His eyebrows knit tighter. "This curse is about to get worse."

My whole body freezes. "What do you mean, worse? Isn't this a good luck charm?" My fingers tighten around the coin that had gleamed so brightly just moments before. Its gold sheen seems dull now.

Ramon shakes his head. "Quite the opposite. This magic is . . . complicated." His eyes flicker to the floor. "The curse's spirits have cast their ill wishes toward the Ruizes since my day. But now, by awakening the anting-anting, you've riled them up." He meets my gaze again, and the intensity in his eyes makes me want to shrink back against the stall door. "I can feel their rage, like someone has thrown a log onto an already blazing fire. You've reminded them that they're angry. And you've given them a target. Freddie: you must be careful."

A wave of dizziness washes over me. Of course breaking a century-long curse wouldn't be as easy as switching on a charm by accident.

But at least there *is* a way to end this curse for good, according to Ramon. I try to push out a confident, I'll-be-fine laugh, but it comes out sounding hollow. "I already have bad luck. What's a few more paper cuts and pop quizzes?"

His lips purse, as if he's holding in some words of pity. His silence at my attempt at a joke makes me feel ten times worse.

When he speaks again, his dark tone makes my knees falter. "Before, the spirits may have been out to annoy, to make your life a little harder. But make no mistake: they will now be out for blood too."

A whistle blows somewhere outside, and it takes me a second to register it against the ominous roar in my ears. My time is almost up. I shove the amulet into my pocket, and Ramon's projection snuffs out like a candle flame. I dash into the locker room, already yanking my collared shirt over my head.

Ramon's warning about my luck repeats in my head like a commercial I can't click away from. And not only am I late to PE class—punished with an extra lap around the track —but I don't realize until afterward that I put my shorts on backwards.

FOUR

THIS CURSE IS ABOUT TO GET WORSE.

I grip my family tree board so tightly it might snap in half.

Nothing life-altering happened during the rest of PE. I'm not sure how much to believe a boy whom I might have entirely hallucinated. Still, I sidle extra carefully down the narrow aisle between desks to my seat in social studies. I watch where I place each footstep, dodging backpack straps, long legs, and patchy parts of the putrid green carpet.

The bell rings, and it's as jarring as Ramon's words from earlier. Every part of our bizarre conversation has been echoing in my mind. A trapped great-granduncle? Evil spirits? A way to actually break the curse? I don't know how I'm going to get through the rest of the school day trying to process this chaos.

On my desk ahead, I spy a yellow card. An invitation to a birthday party. My mood lifts.

Until I hear a whisper across the room. "You invited Faceplant Freddie too?"

It's Dale, the Wyld Beasts crew captain and Sharkey's I-swear-he's-not-that-bad friend. But she's not the one who has to sit through the giggles and snorts of the kids sitting around Dale, like the laugh track in some awful middle school sitcom.

I earned that Faceplant Freddie nickname five years ago, when I splatted off the stage at the second-grade Christmas pageant. I seem to re-earn it every year with some kind of stumble or smack into a wall, flagpole, tree, or ultraclean glass window.

Most recently was my first and last attempt to audition for Sharkey's Wyld Beasts crew. Sharkey's always made her crew friends sound so enviably close, and their choreography doesn't involve any equipment I could accidentally collide with. I nailed the audition, but then my shoelace came untied at the end, and I tripped three other members on my way down to the ground.

Unfortunately for me, no one at Holy Redeemer is ever going to forget that nickname, and no one wants a kid called Faceplant on their team, squad, or circle.

Arturo, the birthday boy, only started at Holy Redeemer

this year, though. "My mom said to invite everyone in the class."

Dale snickers. "But didn't you hear about Benjamin's ninth birthday?"

I can't reach my desk fast enough. I don't want to listen to the story they're telling. Benjamin's party ended with a game of Red Light, Green Light that had me colliding with his mom as she was bringing out the homemade birthday cake. I've said "no, thanks," to everything from there on out, to save myself the embarrassment (and to spare any future homemade birthday cakes). Eventually, the invitations stopped. But the whispers didn't. They're still happening across the classroom, and I don't think my brown face could get any redder.

If I had tight crew bonds like Sharkey has with her friends, maybe I'd be able to grumble about this with someone, to unload some of this icky feeling. Usually, I'm perfectly happy with just my Robo-Warrior card collection, but those aren't exactly friends. And cards can't stand up for me when people are being rude.

Breaking this curse could strip away some of this clumsiness.

Breaking this curse could mean me shedding the Faceplant nickname once and for all.

Breaking the curse could change everything.

Mr. Zhou closes the classroom door and clicks the pen in his hand. "For those of you who weren't here for the announcement" — he's trying to be nice, but he's clearly looking straight at me, because I'm not even seated yet — "drop off your boards at the side table."

A quick glance around confirms that no one else has their family tree boards at their desks. Everyone's projects are on the long plastic table, at the far corner from where I'm standing.

Now I'm all too aware of the fact that I, the only one clutching my project, have the entire class's eyes on me.

To avoid turning and beaning anyone with my backpack, walking backwards seems like my best option. So I place one foot behind the other and begin to inch toward the aisle opening at the front of the classroom. And because I'm still facing the class, I get to see everyone's amused smirks as they watch me squirm.

Ramon's warning to be alert is still fresh, so I maneuver warily around those obstacles I bypassed on my way in. The corner of Dale's overstuffed canvas backpack, Layla's paper-bag-covered social studies book, Arturo's wadded-up hoodie.

I'm getting close to the front of the class now. Only a few more steps, a swift turn, and a skip over to the side table to turn in this board.

A quick shadow to my left catches my eye. It looks like an arm, and I worry that someone's getting up from their desk. I angle right to give them room, but my foot catches on something.

My legs buckle beneath me. I stagger back, trying to correct my balance, but all I manage is to whirl around wildly as I begin to fall.

My knees thud hard against the thin-carpeted ground. My skull narrowly misses a sharp desk edge. Then a loud crunch blasts through my ears and into my bones.

The air is sucked out of the classroom as the entire class gasps.

For a second, I don't move. Because if I get up, that really means that I've just fallen on my face—again—in front of the whole classroom. At this rate, I'll be Faceplant Freddie when I'm ninety.

Mr. Zhou helps me up. "Are you all right, Freddie?"

Besides the throbbing knees and my already bruised dignity, nothing's hurt. I dust my pants off and nod, then notice Mr. Zhou's worried brown eyes aren't on me. They're on my family tree board, which is on the floor. In fact, everyone's staring at my board. Even Sharkey, who's used to this kind of clumsiness from me, has her jaw ajar enough for me to see her cavity fillings.

I glance down at the wreck that used to be a B-or-higher-grade assignment. The weight of my fall has folded my board in half and flattened it, like a cardboard quesadilla. Scattered around it are crumpled leaves and neatly written labels that I painstakingly superglued in place last night.

My heart plunges into my stomach with a sickening splash. Not just because my social studies grade is in jeopardy, but because Ramon's words practically scream out in my brain.

This curse is about to get worse.

FIVE

I GRAB MY LUNCH BAG OUT OF MY LOCKER, AND A WHIFF OF
Dad's garlic fried rice floats out. But instead of my usual
mouth-water reaction, my mouth still feels dry, like I've eaten
a bucket of sand. The breakfast leftovers I'd been so excited
about this morning suddenly seem less thrilling.

The fall in Mr. Zhou's class brought forth a fresh wave
of Faceplant Freddie mentions, and I shudder to think about
how long it's going to take everyone to stop talking about it
this time. I stuff Arturo's yellow birthday party invitation
into my locker. Even if his mom didn't force him to invite
me, he likely doesn't want me showing up now. It's better for
everyone if my cursed butt stays home.

Red-painted lockers clang shut around me, and the hallway begins to empty. Kids are spreading throughout the

school for lunch—the cafeteria, the six concrete tables out-side usually taken up by eighth-graders, the grassy space in the quad. But I'm focusing instead on where I can hide out for the next forty minutes.

Part of me wants to seek out my usual Tuesday lunch-time gathering—the super secret Robo-Warrior battle group on the south side of the gym. They're one of the few groups at school that welcome almost anyone, as long as you can answer their obscure Robo-Warrior trivia questions. I haven't gotten a single one wrong. But I know Dale and a few other kids from my class sometimes show up with their card decks, too, and I have no desire to see their pitying—or worse, still-laughing—faces.

A voice floats up to my ears. "I told you so."

I peer around to make sure no one's looking my way, then fish the amulet out of my pocket.

Ramon projects himself out next to me, leaning up against a locker.

"What are you doing?" I whisper harshly. "Someone will notice you!"

Just then Layla strolls straight through Ramon and opens her locker.

"She doesn't see you," I mutter.

I should've remembered she could hear me, though. Layla turns her head slowly, tucks one of her twists behind her ear, and flashes me a friendly, but concerned, smile. "You okay, Freddie?"

I force a series of rough coughs and bring the crook of my elbow up to cover my mouth. "Yeah, I just"—another fake cough—"my throat."

Layla nods sympathetically as she deposits a couple textbooks. Meanwhile, Ramon projects himself next to her and waves his arms and sticks out his tongue. His mouth twists in disappointment when he realizes a limitation to his abilities.

As Layla juggles her books, one slips from her grasp and tumbles to the ground. I reach to catch it but instead tip it off course. It lands squarely on my own foot.

I bite back a yelp and ignore Ramon's laughter as I pick up the book and hand it to her.

"Thanks," she says, tucking the textbook away and closing her locker. "You sure everything's all right? That fall in Mr. Zhou's class looked pretty intense."

I nod and clench my fists to distract from my throbbing foot and chuckling Ramon. "I'm fine. I've been through worse."

She smiles because she knows it's true but doesn't want to say it out loud. She's nice, unlike Ramon, who apparently decides it's the time to test out more of his ghost abilities by trying to poke Layla in the eye.

"Stop it!" I snap.

The smile drops from her face as Ramon breaks out into a fresh peal of laughter.

"That settles it. She can't see, hear, or feel me. But you, on the other hand . . ." He doubles over and slaps his thigh.

I scramble for a creative, believable explanation but come up short. I force a cough again. "Something stuck"—fake cough—"throat."

She nods, the pinch of her eyebrows the only sign that this wasn't a normal conversation, and walks away. It's easier for both of us to pretend that I didn't do something weird. Twice.

I wait until she's out of sight to speak to Ramon again. "Why can't she sense you?"

He shrugs and wipes a tear from under his eye. "Perhaps because she doesn't believe in this kind of magic."

Mom and Dad won't be able to see him, then, if he decides to make an appearance at home.

"Then can you at least not bug me while I'm around people? I'm not exactly Mr. Popular as it is."

"I'm still learning what the bounds of this anting-anting are. It is not my fault you do not know when to hold your tongue. You should be more careful."

I sputter, trying to form a response. I do not need Who Talks to Himself added to my nickname today.

The grin still on his face, Ramon strolls casually away from the wall of lockers.

"What are you so happy about?" I bark. "You're cursed, too."

"Yes, but now I have you to help me break it! I can tell you what I know of this magic, and you can—well, you can just do everything I say."

His smile widens, and my own scowl deepens. I have a sudden urge to chuck this amulet and the snarky great-granduncle in it down the hallway.

The sight of a deep notch carved into the edge of the coin stops me. It looks like someone hacked into it with a blade and nicked out a tiny piece.

"What is this?" I scratch at the notch with my thumbnail, in case it's just a bit of dirt, but it doesn't come off or smooth down. "Did I mess this up when I fell?"

The joy vanishes from Ramon's face. His voice goes serious. "Oh no, Freddie. The countdown. It has begun."

I almost groan. "Fine, I'll bite. What countdown?"

"A notch will appear on this coin each day. It seems to be the curse's spirits' way of keeping time. Of tracking the days they haunt and harm you."

I turn the amulet over in my hands. One notch already. I think back to what's happened to me in the half day that's passed since I activated the amulet at Mass. The backwards shorts, tripping, the demolished board, the toe-crushing textbook.

"So what, they scratch up this coin to keep count? I've had bad luck pretty much every day of my life. At some point, there won't be any coin left."

I end with a snort of laughter, but Ramon doesn't seem to think that's funny.

"You only get thirteen notches, Freddie. That means thirteen days' worth of bad luck. When I got the anting-anting, my bootlaces kept untying, my compass broke, my weapon jammed . . ." He gulps. "It has been so long since the curse's anger was aimed at me that I'd forgotten just how quickly those spirits work. We need to break the curse before the spirits carve that thirteenth notch."

A shiver runs down my back. "Why? What happens on the thirteenth day?"

He pauses for a moment, like he doesn't want to tell me. Then he sighs, and the word that comes out is spoken so low I almost don't hear it. "Death."

My jaw and my lunch bag drop to the floor.

"Are you kidding me?" I shriek. My heart rate spikes to a thousand beats a minute. "Death? I'm only twelve!"

It's then that I notice a group of sixth-grade girls down the hallway. They point at me and chuckle among themselves.

I don't even try to pretend my yelling at the empty space in front of me wasn't weird. I wave at them, which sends them sprinting to the cafeteria, laughing.

I need to get out of this very public hallway. I swipe my lunch bag off the speckled linoleum and dart toward the nearest exit. The heavy door empties me out next to the cafeteria dumpsters, already starting to reek under the noon sun. The whole area smells faintly of old bananas and dried-up milk.

Ramon's projection trails behind me.

"So I've only got twelve more days of bad luck before I—" I can't even say "die" out loud. Is that seriously how this curse ends? I might die before I'm old enough to vote, to drive, to watch a PG-13 movie with friends (hypothetically, if I had friends)? I might not even last long enough to know what grade I got on my family tree board.

Ramon's projection flickers away, and when I look down at the coin, he's back inside. "I died thirteen days after I angered the spirits. We cannot let the spirits kill you. If you die, you will get trapped in here with me, and then who will free us?"

The threat of dying was bad enough, but adding the punishment of spending eternity with this pushy ghost? I need this curse gone.

Some heavy steps lumber in my direction, and I leap

out of the way just as one of the cafeteria workers heaves a stained cardboard box into the dumpster. Rancid bits of shredded lettuce rain down on me anyway.

In the coin, Ramon laughs as I flick the lettuce shreds out of my hair. I pause, staring at the green flecks on the asphalt beneath me. This isn't lettuce.

"It's moldy cheese!" I screech.

Ramon's laughter grows more obnoxious.

I lean over and shake, like a wet dog, casting off the last of the cheese.

"I don't want thirteen days of worse luck, and I definitely don't want to join you in that amulet death jail. Tell me exactly what I have to do to get rid of this bad luck once and for all."

"Well, that's part of the mission." Ramon rubs the back of his neck in a way that makes me think he's not as big of an overconfident know-it-all as he seems. "I don't know precisely how to break this curse. Your first task will be finding out."

SIX

TRYING TO CONCENTRATE ON A POP QUIZ IN MATH CLASS while a ghost peeks over my shoulder making tsk-tsk noises was definitely *not* in today's plans. I lower my eyelids and blow out a slow breath, just like I've seen on Mom's yoga videos.

"You should concentrate on your quiz, not take a nap," Ramon says.

My eyelids snap open. "Leave me alone," I whisper as quietly as I can.

Ramon juts a finger at my quiz paper. "There. That should be a two, not a three."

My hands clench into fists. "I got this."

"Clearly you do not 'got' this if your answer is wrong." He spits my words back at me like they're old candy.

A surge of anger channels into my hands, and my wooden pencil snaps in half.

I didn't have the stomach to eat lunch after discovering that this curse was going to kill me off in twelve days. Then I dragged myself back into the classroom, hungry and super stressed out, only to have this pop quiz sprung on me.

Ramon is only getting increasingly annoying. He's become bored sitting in the amulet while I'm in class. Since lunch, he's already asked two dozen questions that I can't answer out loud. I shouldn't even be shushing him now, in case someone accuses me of cheating on this quiz.

The teacher announces, "All right, class. Finish up and pass your papers to the front." She's been pacing around the classroom keeping an eye on all of us, her leather boots squeaking with each slow step.

I speed through the last two problems on the page with my broken pencil. Ramon shakes his head at me as I hand my paper forward.

"You answered that last question wrong."

"Well, I was rushing because *somebody* wouldn't leave me alone," I snarl. "Besides, you could've been a little more helpful. You could've just told me the answers."

"But then how would you learn?" he says with a grin.

Why couldn't a less obnoxious family member have been cursed and trapped in the amulet?

I'm exhausted by the time the end-of-the-day bell rings. Sharkey's already at the curbside pickup line when I head outside. I weave through the clusters of waiting kids, the flustered teachers' assistants trying to herd hyper students, and the parents trying to juggle backpacks and cell phones and art projects. A couple high-pitched third-graders are singing off-key and playing a hand-clapping game. Each note is like a kick to the eardrums.

I make it to Sharkey. "You riding home with us today? I thought you were going to the skate park with Misa."

Sharkey blows out a breath, sending her bangs fluttering over her forehead, and readjusts the backpack straps on her shoulders. "Dad said I could only go if you were going."

A familiar jab of guilt hits my chest. *Only if Freddie goes* is Uncle Sammy's sneaky way of saying, *No way. Too dangerous, risky, or inappropriate for Sharlene!* He knows I avoid anything even remotely hazardous, and poor Sharkey's paid the price.

Sharkey shoots a sideways look at me. "And let me guess: you don't want to risk cracking your head open falling off a skateboard?"

I nod. She knows me too well. Our whole lives, the curse has managed to spoil all my fun and much of hers. She doesn't hate me for it—we get along fine when it's just us hanging out or with our families—but I don't really blame her for avoiding me at school. It's probably not fun being associated with me. And top it off with the fact that I'm her father's favorite excuse for saying no? Actually, it's amazing she ever puts up with me.

"It's all right," she says with a dismissive wave as Dad's truck pulls up. "After your spill in class, I'd hate to see you on wheels. Plus I've got Spring Showcase soon and should probably get in the extra dance practice."

"Maybe next time," I offer out of guilt.

"Yeah, maybe."

We both know I won't go next time either.

Sharkey slides into the backseat first, and I pile in after her. I almost gag on the sharp smell of Dad's new pine-scented car freshener.

"Hi, Uncle Vic," Sharkey sings in her overly cheerful tone.

I roll my eyes. Leave it to Sharkey to one-up me in manners. To my own father.

Dad smiles warmly into the rearview mirror. "Hi, Sharlene. Freddie, good news: the dentist had a last-minute cancellation, so we rescheduled your appointment for this afternoon."

I'm about to complain—because really, how is that good news, Dad?—but then stop myself. I don't need his anger laser-beamed at me, especially when I've got secret supernatural-related sleuthing to do later tonight. My plan is to stay awake long after Mom and Dad go to sleep so I can steal an hour of unauthorized internet time on Dad's laptop. I have to learn everything I can about anting-anting, curses, spirits, and ghostly projections.

I pull out my favorite pen—a blue Robo-Warrior one I got for my birthday—and a piece of torn notebook paper I've been taking notes on as ideas cross my mind. I scrawl down a couple more reminders on what to Google after this surprise trip to the dentist. And on the low-tech side, Apong Rosing might be able to provide some pointers.

That's when I see it again, that shadow right at the edge of my vision. I swivel to face it, but focusing on the shadow is impossible. One moment I think I see a hand, but then I blink and nothing seems weird or out of place. Just the usual hordes of kids waiting on the sidewalk for their rides.

I ignore the quickening thump in my chest. All this talk of bad luck and spirits must be hyper-stimulating my imagination.

Dad fiddles with his phone to put on his afternoon podcast, and I try to blow my unease out with another slow yoga breath.

I go to click my pen closed, and it explodes, spraying blue

ink everywhere. My thumb catches an exposed metal edge of the pen, and the skin slices open. A drop of red mingles with the blue on my hand.

Sharkey scoots away faster than I've ever seen her move.

The blue ink, tinged with blood, seeps onto my hands and all over my white uniform shirt.

From the front seat, Dad looks like he's about to erupt. "Quick, wipe it up before it messes up the seats!" He tosses a dirty shop towel at me. It smacks me right on the forehead.

I wipe my inky hands off on the towel and my already blue-smeared shirt. The ink ruins the rabbit's foot keychain on my backpack. I guess it isn't so lucky after all.

Snickers trickle in from outside, and I realize, with horror, that a couple kids have spotted me. I slink down in the seat, my shirt mopping up stray specks of ink from the leather. I know I've got bigger things to worry about—like possible doom in twelve days—but I have no interest in taking on a new nickname (Freddie Kahlo?).

"Dad, let's go!" I urge. I raise the shop towel to shield my face from the growing audience.

Then I realize that this isn't some old shop towel. I'm clutching a pair of faded, holey plaid *boxers*. And now everyone on the sidewalk has seen me wipe my face with underwear.

I launch them into the front seat. "Dad, gross! Are these

yours?" Of course they are. He never throws anything away. That's why our garage-cave is the way it is. Dad will find a way to repurpose something until it decays into dust.

Dad rolls his eyes at me. "Come on, Freddie. Cloth is cloth. Everything cleaned up back there?"

I grumble a yes and slink down even further. The thin cut on my thumb has already stopped bleeding. My sense of pride, battered as it is, will take much longer to recover.

Once Dad is satisfied that I haven't destroyed the seats, he shifts the truck into drive and pulls away from the curb. He cranks up the volume on his true crime podcast and proceeds to tune us out for the fifteen-minute ride home.

I don't understand how Dad doesn't believe in the Ruiz family curse: his luck is just as bad as mine. His shoelaces come untied so often he has to special-order Velcro-strap work boots. Every time he bets more than twenty bucks on a basketball team, they lose miserably. And when the construction company he worked for since I was born announced layoffs two years ago, somehow he was the only one in his team cut out of a job.

His brother, my Uncle Ritchie, shares the same awful luck. They have the same dark brown skin, stocky build, and serious eyes, but Uncle Ritchie sports a goatee and a thick ponytail. (Dad's balding. It's best not to mention that or the curse to him, ever.) Like Apong Rosing, Uncle Ritchie's a firm believer in what Dad dismisses as "nonsense." Uncle Ritchie has invested loads of time and money into anyone and anything promising to banish his sorry luck. On his regular business trips to the Philippines, he treks around making offerings at every church or holy site rumored to bring good fortune.

The curse pestered their father, and Apong Rosing's only son, my Grandpa Carlo, too. His previous cars, without fail, would end up clobbered by fallen tree branches during every winter storm, back when he lived in Chicago.

My guess is Dad's in denial about all this stuff because he's seen how wacky it can make people. I think he's afraid I'll turn out like Uncle Ritchie.

I wait until Dad's focused on driving and murder to pull the amulet out of my pocket. "Those spirits are out for blood, all right. How much worse is this going to get?" I groan.

"Um, Freddie? Who are you talking to?"

It takes a second for me to remember that Sharkey's in the backseat too. And now she's seen me speak to a coin. I cringe.

She raises an eyebrow, and the excuses die on my tongue. She's always been able to see through my attempts at lies. I'd have a better chance at convincing my parents to quit their jobs and move us to another continent rather than trying to fib my way out of this.

From the coin, Ramon lets out a pointed cough. "Ahem. He was talking to me."

The blood drains from poor Sharkey's face. "You've got to be kidding me."

I lean toward her. "You can hear him too?"

She nods slowly, then rubs her eyes like this is all some trick of the afternoon light.

So she really must believe in this Filipino magic.

"He's real," I whisper. "Unfortunately."

"No way." She shakes her head. "I've seen these kinds of toys on TV. It's got, like, fifty preprogrammed responses and will tell you the time or the temperature and stuff, right?"

Ramon laughs. "Why would you ask a coin the time? Have you no wristwatch?"

Sharkey's jaw drops.

"See?" I tilt the coin at her. "What kind of weird kids' toy would be programmed to say 'wristwatch'?"

"I . . ." She shuts her mouth, then glares at me as if her disbelief is my fault. "Give me that." She snatches the coin and brings it up to her eye level.

Ramon's head dips slightly in acknowledgment. "Pleased to meet you."

Sharkey's mouth moves like she's about to say something, but she swallows her words. Her eyes stay as wide as headlights as she shoves the coin back at me.

To my relief, Ramon stays in the amulet instead of giving Sharkey the same brain-busting scare he gave me earlier. "Are all children your age so rude to your elders?"

"You have to give us some time to accept this. Sharkey's taking it much better than I did. I almost dropped you in the toilet."

Ramon pinches the bridge of his nose like talking to me is headache-inducing. "Freddie, we must focus. Your hand. When you get home, you must clean it properly so it does not become infected. The curse is only going to get worse."

Death countdown aside, it would be really tough to shuffle a Robo-Warrior card deck with an infected thumb. I reach for the pack of tissues at the bottom of my backpack.

"It's . . . it's really talking," Sharkey sputters.

I flash her a sympathetic smile. I'm sure I appeared far more frazzled when Ramon first snapped at me before PE class.

"That's Ramon, my great-granduncle on my dad's side," I explain quietly. "He died in World War II. Then the curse trapped him in here."

This time, Ramon projects a hand out of the coin to give a polite wave. Sharkey nearly melts out of her seat.

She doesn't seem like she's going to be able to form words anytime soon, so I push Ramon for more info. "Later tonight, I'm going to start searching for a way to break this curse. Is there anything you can think of that might help?"

"This anting-anting"—Ramon waves his hands at the gold all around him—"it actually belongs to my best friend, Ingo Agustin. If you find him, maybe he can tell us how to get rid of the curse."

"Wait. Your best friend? What if he's still in the Philippines?"

"And World War II," Sharkey croaks. "That was, like, a hundred years ago, wasn't it? What if he's dead?"

Ramon scoffs. "It wasn't a hundred years ago. Ingo may still be alive, but I don't know where. And I can't get to him myself."

I thump my head on the cushioned car seat in front of me. In addition to all the homework on my to-do list tonight, I have to track down a man in his ninety-somethings. I highly doubt this Ingo would be on any social media.

Sharkey nudges my shoe with hers. "Hey, I'll help you," she whispers.

"Really?" I angle my head to face her. "But this curse doesn't affect you. You're not a Ruiz."

She offers a weak smile. "We're next-door neighbors, we go to the same school, and we carpool. The last thing I need is for evil spirits to drag an asteroid down on both our heads."

She has a point. And I'm not going to turn down help, especially when I'm not a hundred percent sure where to even start. The thought of having an ally—a non-ghost one —lifts my mood. "Thanks. I'll come over after my dentist appointment, and we can Google this Ingo guy. You know my parents and their screen restrictions."

Sharkey shakes her head. "No, I like my computer the way it is: working. And it's off-limits, thanks to your dad teaching my dad some new parental control app. I'll come over to your house instead. We'll figure out a plan of attack. Don't be offended if I bring a helmet, okay?"

I laugh. But to be honest, I'm not at all sure she was joking.

SEVEN

SHARKEY DOESN'T, IN FACT, WEAR A HELMET OVER TO our house. But, as I fill her in on the details of this newest twist of the curse, she does check the legs of my desk chair before she lowers herself onto it.

I'm sitting cross-legged on my bed, clutching a pillow and staring at the amulet, bright against the faded blue bedsheet.

There's room for Sharkey if she wanted to join me in taking a closer peek at the amulet. But as she stated as soon as she walked in, my room is a pigsty, and there's no way she's jumping right into the mud. The plain wooden desk chair seemed the least disgusting option to her.

"What are we waiting for?" Sharkey asks, finally satisfied that her seat isn't going to collapse underneath her. She leans left to peek down the hallway and into the living room. She's checking on Apong Rosing, who's at her regularly scheduled seat on the couch, focused on her soap operas, her teleserye. She hasn't moved in the twelve minutes since the episode began. The house could be on fire and my great-grandmother would still insist on finishing her show.

"A commercial break," Ramon answers from the amulet. He projects himself next to me on the bed, mimicking my cross-legged position. Then he sneers down at the pajamas balled up next to me and projects a few inches further away.

Sharkey straightens. "No offense, but how do you even know about television and commercial breaks? Haven't you been stuck in that thing since the 1940s?"

Ramon purses his lips and folds his arms, a motion I've seen Apong do a thousand times. He's offended. "I can still see out of the coin. Before Freddie's father stuck me in a drawer, I got to see such wondrous things as the Nintendo and the microwave oven and pocket-size telephones that fold in half."

I catch the hint of sadness that weaves into the end of Ramon's sentence. Ramon was just a teenager when he died. There is so much he missed out on. Sure, he was able to see some of it from his prison in the amulet, but he couldn't join in or even talk to anyone until I came along.

I shush them as I try to home in on the sound of the television. I am thrilled to discover that my dentist-caused facial numbness is almost gone. It was torture listening to Ramon ooh and aah over all the shiny dental instruments while I was stuck with my mouth stretched open. I wish the dentist had just knocked me out instead.

The TV music ramps up dramatically, which means there will probably be some big gaspworthy moment before they go to commercial. "The plan is to ask her about Ingo," I say, and Sharkey nods.

Ramon stands and starts to pace. He's probably not only nervous about Ingo, but about speaking to his sister for the first time in decades. Apong was napping when I got home from school. I had to convince Ramon it wasn't a good idea for a ghost brother to surprise a groggy eighty-seven-year-old who's on all sorts of heart medications.

"He's the most likely person to be able to tell us how to break this curse," Ramon says.

Sharkey frowns. "If he's still alive."

"And if Apong remembers him," I add.

After such a long day, it's hard not to be negative. Especially when the way out of this mess starts with locating a man almost a century old, last seen half a world away. And if he died a long time ago? There might not even be a bread crumb anywhere online about him.

Apong Rosing is our best starting point. She regularly calls her cousin's daughter Nita back in the Philippines, in their town of Santa Maria. I know from my family tree board that generations of Ruizes lived in Santa Maria before coming here to the United States as service members, spouses, or nurses.

"Ingo and I were more than ten years older than Rosita," Ramon explains. "Ingo was eighteen, but I was seventeen when we went to join the Philippine Scouts, a special unit of the United States Army. It was Filipinos alongside American officers. Rosita would have been six years old then. I don't know how much she would truly remember of us. And I don't know if or when Ingo would have returned home after the war."

We need Apong's knowledge. And if anyone's going to understand that I'm helping her trapped brother break the family curse, it's going to be her.

It's almost time for that commercial break. I grab the amulet. Instead of putting it in my pocket, I sling the leather cord around my neck. "That way you can see what's going on," I tell Ramon.

Ramon chuckles. "Thank you. I was getting tired of seeing all the dirt and lint in your pockets. You should tell your laundress to be more thorough."

Sharkey and I stroll into the living room right as the commercials begin. Sharkey scrunches her face at the over-enthusiastic skin-whitening cream ad on the screen. The beauty obsession with lighter skin weirds us out. I'd probably melt all my skin off if I ever accidentally used one of those products.

The orange light from the TV casts a warm glow over everything in the dim living room, Apong Rosing included. She sits in the center of the lumpy beige couch we've had since I was a toddler. A bright line of magenta crayon runs up its right side, which Mom shoved a white end table against to cover up. Apong's crossword puzzle and pen sit atop that table, along with a stack of tabloid magazines and the TV remote, all taped up to keep the batteries from falling out.

I cross Apong's line of sight of the television to plop down next to her. The couch squeaks under my added weight. Sharkey sits on the other side. We have Apong Rosing surrounded.

Apong tugs her purple cardigan, the one she always wears to the dialysis center, tightly around her thin frame, then gives a heavy, exaggerated sigh as she realizes she has company. I'd be more offended if I didn't need her cooperation so much.

"Apong," I start, "can we ask you about Santa Maria after World War II?"

Instantly suspicious, she narrows her eyes at me. "Why?"

"School project," Sharkey blurts out.

"Ah." Apong Rosing's face softens with a smile. She adores Sharkey—a model student! Such a polite girl! Not like me, the troublemaker, in Apong's eyes. Apong should understand that it's the curse that causes trouble, not me —she's a cursed Ruiz too. It's not like I set her crossword puzzle book on fire on purpose last year. And I even snuffed out the flames for her.

I nod at Sharkey, urging her to continue.

"We're learning about the Rescission Act, right after the war," Sharkey says, the cover story easy on her lips. She's way too good at this.

Apong Rosing shakes her head. "Ah, yes. So upsetting, for the US government to break the promises it made to Filipinos for their military service. They told Filipino soldiers they would receive the same benefits as other American veterans. But the Rescission Act took those benefits away."

"That's awful. Your brother fought in the war, didn't he?" I ask.

The corners of Apong's mouth dip. "Yes, he did. A lot of the boys in our town went to fight."

The next commercial comes on. We don't have much time. We'll lose Apong's attention the second the broad-shouldered love interest flashes back on the screen.

I gesture to the amulet around my neck. "This anting-anting. Did a lot of the boys have these?"

"I don't know what this has to do with your Filipino veterans project." Apong's lips purse. "But now that I think of it, my brother's friend Ingo did. This anting-anting looks very much like his."

My jaw nearly drops at the mention of Ingo, but it hits the rug when Ramon projects out in front of us. Exactly what I'd told him not to do.

"You remember Ingo!" he shouts excitedly.

I don't think I've ever seen Apong Rosing speechless, but here we are, her mouth open so wide a bee could buzz in and out of it. Music and flashing lights stream out of the television, but she's not even paying it the slightest bit of attention. Her eyes are squarely on her brother.

A few seconds later, she croaks, "But . . . you . . . how?"

"I've been trapped in this anting-anting!"

"This whole time?"

Ramon nods. "Yes! I was with you, Rosita. When you said goodbye to our parents in Santa Maria, when you scolded your boy, Carlo, for his poor grades, when you flew here to America with too many bags to help him care for Ritchie and Victor."

Ramon's voice wavers, and I feel my own throat go tight.

On Apong Rosing's face, I watch the teary-eyed shock turn into something softer, then into red-hot anger.

She reaches past me, snatches her crossword puzzle book

off the end table, rolls it up, and swats at Ramon's projection. The book goes right through him, but he flinches anyway.

"Ramon!" she shrieks. "You almost gave me a heart attack!"

"Aren't you glad to—"

She swats again. "What were you thinking, appearing out of nowhere like this and screaming at me?"

Sharkey and I exchange glances. This sibling reunion is going about as well as we could've hoped for.

"If you've been with me this whole time, you should have known how many pills I'm taking!" Apong says with a scowl.

"Rosita, focus!" Ramon says, pushing his forearm out in front of him, like he could (or even needed to) block her blows. "What happened to Ingo?"

Apong's brow stays tight, but she at least unrolls her crossword puzzle book and sets it in her lap. "What did you get these children involved in, Ramon?"

"Ramon thinks Ingo can help us break the curse," I say.

She turns her fiery glare on me. "So there is no school project? That was a lie?"

Sharkey switches on her most innocent smile. "We were hoping to get the information more gently, without giving you that heart attack."

Apong nods at Sharkey in thanks. Typical that Sharkey would somehow get painted the good kid in all of this.

"Ingo was from one of the wealthier families in our town," Apong says. "The Agustins owned a rice mill. It burned down during the war. Ingo came home for a little while after the fighting was done, and I saw him around town once or twice. But with the mill gone, his family had nothing. They moved away."

I scoot an inch closer. "Do you know where we can find him and his family?"

Apong shakes her head. "No. I don't know where they moved to."

My hopes deflate, and Ramon's projection flickers. That's definitely not the answer we want.

"Maybe we can look him up," Sharkey says. "He or his kids might be on Facebook or something, and we can—"

Apong cuts her off with the wave of her hand. The soap opera title splays across the screen, and the love interest is about to burst into the beautiful main character's apartment to profess his devotion. "Later, later," Apong mumbles, dismissing us. "If I don't watch this episode, the ladies at the dialysis center will spoil it for me. Go play somewhere."

Sharkey shoots me an "is she serious?" look.

"But Apong, the curse, it's—"

"Take them outside, Ramon," she orders, as if Ramon's a living, breathing adult who can grab us by the arms and haul us away.

Ramon's eyes go distant for a moment, as if he's gazing at something that we can't see, then he nods firmly. "Yes, let's go, Freddie. Quickly."

I sigh and motion for Sharkey to follow me outside. We're not going to get much else out of Apong Rosing until this show's over.

Sharkey swings the front door open, and we step out into the chilly night air.

"The curse's spirits . . . they are watching. I felt them back there, in the living room," Ramon says.

I gulp.

"We cannot involve Rosita in this," he adds, using the same tone of voice that Dad grounds me with.

My stomach dips. I need to break this curse to save myself and my family, and giving up a potential ally seems like a bad idea. "But Apong knows a lot of this magic and folklore stuff. She's going to want to help us break the curse."

Ramon's brow tightens. "We cannot let her. We may ask simple things of her, like we did today. But anything more will put her in danger."

Sharkey crosses her arms. "Excuse me, I didn't get a big

warning about danger when I offered to help. Is it because I'm a Mendoza and not a Ruiz?"

"Precisely. We do not know if the spirits even have the power to affect you," Ramon says. "And you are young, strong. But Rosita? I will make myself clear: we must not draw the spirits' attention to my sister."

Sharkey and I exchange looks: we both know he's right. I think of my stumble in class earlier today. Only my project and my reputation were damaged, but that kind of fall could be a lot worse for someone Apong's age. I don't know what kind of trouble these spirits have in store for us, but none of us want to make her a target.

We nod, and the tension eases out of Ramon's face. It's been decades since he could even talk to his little sister and he's still trying to protect her. It makes me the tiniest bit jealous, like when I see Sharkey and her Wyld Beasts crew.

I turn to Sharkey. "I'll try to sneak some laptop time later and search for Ingo Agustin online. See if we can track him down."

"I'm good at tracking," Ramon says proudly. "I can help. I once found the mayor's carabao after it was missing for three days."

Sharkey laughs. "It's not that kind of tracking, Ramon. Searching online is just typing stuff into a computer and getting information back."

He huffs, unimpressed, and Sharkey starts down the walkway to her home.

I step back inside and lock the door behind me.

"Let's go back to the living room," Ramon suggests.

I pause. "You just said we can't ask for her help!"

"Correct. And I am not going to."

"So what, you want to apologize to Apong Rosing for almost startling her to death? She's not going to want to talk until after her show, even to you."

"No, it's not that," Ramon says. "As much I miss my sister, she can be a cranky one, and I do not want to get on her bad side. I promise I will save all my catching up until after. She must have much to tell me." Then he stretches up as if he could see over my shoulder. "But first, I want to see what happens in this show!"

EIGHT

STAY UP WAY TOO LATE FOR NOTHING.
My plan for unauthorized time on Dad's non-parental-controlled laptop, scouring the internet for any information on anting-anting, fails miserably. A new season of Mom's favorite baking competition show suddenly became available for streaming online today, of all days. Three hour-long episodes in, I realize she's determined to be awake—and standing between me and the laptop—much, much longer than I am. During my dozenth fake trip to the kitchen to get water and secretly check on Mom, I decide enough is enough.

On the way back to my room, I pluck the amulet from on top of Apong Rosing's oak dresser, next to that mother-of-pearl picture frame. It feels safer for me to keep an eye on it. As Ramon predicted, Apong Rosing spent hours telling her brother all about what he'd missed. Eventually, she nodded off and he disappeared back into his amulet, like exhausted kids at a long overdue sleepover (I assume).

In the harsh light of morning, I realize now I should've left Ramon with Apong Rosing.

Because standing over me, yelling, "Wake up!" at the top of his ghost lungs, is the arm-waving projection of my great-granduncle.

In my panic, I flop out of bed onto the carpet with all the grace of a goldfish escaping its fishbowl.

"What's wrong, Ramon? Is it the spirits?" I pop up into a martial arts stance I'd seen on TV, ready to defend myself. I don't know if spirits are vulnerable to karate chops, but coming up with a plan to combat evil, while I'm still in pajamas and with stale morning breath, is too much to ask.

To my horror, my bedroom fades away, and I'm in another bedroom. Gone are my Robo-Warrior posters and messy closet. Instead, cream-colored walls surround me, with a dark wood door on one side and a window, crisscrossed by a matching dark wood, on the other. A simple desk piled high with textbooks sits next to a slim, neatly made bed.

I scream at the same time Ramon does.

"Why are you screaming?" I shriek as I whip around, my arms poised to chop anything that moves.

"Because it worked!" Ramon pumps his arms in the air.

The other bedroom vanishes, and I find myself safely back in my own room.

"Did you do that? Did we time travel or something?"

"No, no," Ramon says, too casually for how rattled I am. "I am simply able to show you things I remember. Like a movie of my memories. That was my old bedroom. Much cleaner than yours, no?"

My arms drop to my sides. "I'm going back to bed."

"Are you not eager to know what I've learned? I've been testing the bounds of my abilities through the night. But first, how about a 'good morning,' eh? I am your elder. You should greet me."

"Elder? You're seventeen. You've got all those pimples."

Ramon rolls his eyes. "I look seventeen, but I'm over eighty years your senior. You should show me more respect."

He's the one who flew out of the amulet throwing around orders and insulting my haircut. I've been positively pleasant, considering everything. Ramon doesn't get a free pass to Apong-level deference just because he's got a few decades on me.

The sleepy fog in my brain refuses to burp out an appropriately annoyed response, so I at least mutter a "good morning" as I drop back into bed and pull the covers over my head. Right in time for my alarm to go off.

Ramon doesn't stop speaking from the moment I haul myself out of bed for the second time. His research last night? He confirmed that he can't project himself more than a few feet away from the amulet, nor can he actually touch anything. He apparently tested this out by repeatedly trying to slap me while I was fast asleep.

The morning blurs by, and suddenly, a whistle blows and reminds me that I'm supposed to be pretending to play soccer in third-period PE right now. My tired, droopy face goes grumpier. I force my heavy limbs into plodding after my teammates.

It's not that I hate PE. I actually enjoy being outside on these mild sunny days. The breeze smells like grass, and the springtime rays are a nice warm change from the polar classroom with its forever-broken thermostat.

But sports and me? We just don't mix.

When it comes to getting picked for teams, earning a chance at the ball, or simply not slipping on the grass and landing on my butt, I can never catch a break.

Particularly today, when there are evil spirits bent on making me miserable.

"Hurry up, Freddie!" Layla calls from down the soccer field. We're on the same team, so she's wearing a red mesh jersey too. She points to the left of the goal. "Head over there, it's wide open!"

Then Arturo, on the blue team, drives the ball in exactly that direction.

Earlier this year, Arturo encouraged me to try out for the school's soccer team. School had just started, and new kid Arturo hadn't yet heard the tales of Faceplant Freddie. The tryout didn't go well, thanks to a pair of shoes that were a teensy bit too big, and Arturo hasn't spoken to me about soccer—or much else, really—since then. Sad, because I hear he's looking for pointers on Robo-Warrior strategies, and I know—with no exaggeration—a hundred of them. I could've handpicked a couple of the best Robo-Warrior guides as a birthday present, if I had any plans to actually attend his party.

Arturo's legs pump fast, like they're steam-powered, flattening grass under each determined step. Even if I wasn't cursed, I wouldn't have been able to block him in time. I break into a sprint anyway.

With a swift kick, he sends the soccer ball sailing past the red-jerseyed goalkeeper. The blue team erupts in cheers. My team, on the other hand, shoots glares as fiery red as their jerseys in my direction.

"Why don't you get closer?" Ramon says from the amulet dangling around my neck.

I try to ignore him, his unwanted advice, and my angry teammates' stares. I do love soccer and wish I was good enough to play. But anything requiring more than a minute of focused limb-eye coordination is risky. Just last week, during basketball, my one attempt at a three-pointer somehow got the basketball hopelessly wedged between the hoop and the backboard. We had to stop playing so the janitor could prop his ladder up and save the day.

No, I'm safer where I am: far enough to avoid a collision with another player, but close enough that Mrs. Barnes won't dock me participation points.

"I'd rather not," I mumble, careful to avoid drawing any attention to the fact that I look like I'm talking to myself. I squeezed in one ventriloquism video on the way to school this morning, so I think I've got the lips-not-moving thing down. Or at least I hope I do.

"No superstar athletic maneuvers for me, Ramon. You said this curse is going to get worse, and I've only got two notches on this amulet. Two out of thirteen days down. I don't want to test out how much more hazardous my life can get."

I blink, and suddenly Ramon's standing right next to me, staring out at the game. "You can't stay on the sidelines forever."

"I know!" He doesn't need to know that my whole life has been safe sideline sitting. "That's why we have to break this curse. There won't even be a 'forever' for me if we don't figure this all out."

To keep Mrs. Barnes and my teammates happy, I pick up the pace and follow the ball.

Ramon strolls next to me, his feet on the ground but the grass beneath them untouched. "Correction: there will indeed be a 'forever' for you, but it will be one stuck in this amulet jail, if these spirits get their way."

I drag a hand through my hair. There's so much about this mess that I still don't know, and this fuzziness makes me feel helpless. "What else can you tell me about anting-anting, Ramon? Apong Rosing said that an anting-anting loses its power if it's not with its owner. But something's off here: this amulet didn't just lose its power. The power was reversed somehow. The amulet actually brings bad luck."

I practically hear Ramon gulp. "Huh."

My shoes clomp to a stop on the grass. I know that tone. The family-member-is-hiding-something tone that Dad uses to disguise Grandpa Carlo's visits. "Any idea what would've made the anting-anting turn bad?"

"I . . . Who knows?" Ramon stammers.

He must know more than he's letting on.

I drop the ventriloquist act. "Spill it, Ramon."

"Spill what? I don't understand these modern sayings of yours."

I grit my teeth. "Nice try. You know what I mean. How can I break the curse if you don't tell me everything I need to know?"

"I am telling you everything!" he snaps.

Alarms blare out in my brain. There's a question simmering there, one I should have asked at the beginning. I tug the amulet out of my shirt. The two notches glint in the bright sun.

"Wait, this amulet. It's Ingo's," I say carefully. I turn to face Ramon's projection, but he's purposely trying to avoid eye contact with me. "Ramon, how did you get Ingo's amulet in the first place?"

He lowers his head and kicks at the ground. The blades of grass underneath his boots don't move.

"I . . . I stole it."

NINE

*T*HE AMULET FLASHES SO BRIGHTLY I SHUT MY EYES.
When I open them again, gone are the red- and blue-
jerseyed seventh-graders sprinting around me. Instead,
the patchy green grass below fades into a dirt road. Green
fields dotted with tropical trees and thatched-roof farm-
houses lie on either side of us. Even the air feels different.
Not the breezy spring warmth of the soccer field, but a
stickiness that lies thick on my skin.

Ramon has projected his world—the world before he
died—for me. This projection seems much more vivid than
his bedroom one this morning. I feel like I could grab a
handful of the dirt beneath my feet and let it sift through
my fingers.

I clutch the amulet tighter, as if letting go would make
this all disappear. "Where are we now?"

He doesn't meet my gaze. "I need you to understand. I need you to see."

A cloud of dust kicks up in the distance. Something is marching toward us.

"The war wasn't what we thought it'd be," Ramon says. He stares down the road with me at the approaching cloud. "It wasn't all parades and glory and pretty girls waving their handkerchiefs at us. Ingo and I didn't truly know what we were getting into when we enlisted."

"Then why'd you do it in the first place?" I ask. Sweat beads on my nose.

He shoves his hands in his pockets. "It was after the bombing of Pearl Harbor in Hawaii. American and Filipino troops began rolling through the town more often."

I blink. "American troops? What were they doing in Santa Maria?"

He shakes his head. "The Philippines was a territory of the United States back then. Don't they teach you anything in school?"

I decide then to let him do the talking.

He sighs. "Protect your homeland, they said. Stand against the Imperial Japanese forces. We were among the youngest of the Scouts." He shrugs, and his gaze lowers to his black boots. "But even if we were older, I do not think we would have been ready. Not for the bullets that flew at us, the friends that we lost." Or the terror still clouding his eyes.

I open my mouth to console him, but what can I say? I don't have the words to fit what he's gone through. My worst day was a failed Christmas pageant performance—not a war.

The cloud ahead grows close enough that I can make out the outlines of dust-caked trucks. The dark green tarps stretched over their cargo ripple in the hot wind.

"Um, should we get out of the way?" I ask, a tremor in my voice. The trucks barrel toward us.

I know it's a projection and that the trucks will pass right through us, but I edge to the side anyway. Just in case.

Truck after truck flies by. Boxes and bags are packed into some of them, but in others, tired eyes stare out at us from the trucks' open backs. Sweat and dust streak the soldiers' uniforms, and some sport bandages that probably should've been changed days ago. A couple of the men yell to each other, but I don't understand their Tagalog.

When I lock eyes with one boy, time seems to slow down. He's got a stockier, more muscular build than skinny Ramon, and shares the same sharp haircut, the same dark brown complexion. His fingers wrap tightly around a shining gold circle at his chest.

"Is that Ingo?" I ask. I almost cough at the dirt that floats into my mouth. The projection feels so real. It bombards every one of my senses. I'm glad then that I'd gotten out of the way of those trucks.

Ramon nods. "He had his anting-anting, an old coin he found on a riverbed when we were kids. He drilled a hole into it so he could hang it on a leather cord and wear it close to his body at all times. He was convinced that it would protect him from harm throughout the war."

A figure next to Ingo leans forward. It's Ramon. Not the projection, but the real-life one that must have traveled with Ingo down this dirt road decades ago. There's a wild gleam in his exhausted brown eyes: jealousy.

His next words confirm it. "Because Ingo was so certain that this anting-anting would save him, so was I. Low on ammunition? Ingo somehow stumbled upon an extra case of bullets. An enemy ambush? Ingo would walk out without so much as a scratch. Platoon-wide sickness thanks to rotten rations? Ingo slept like a baby, on a full stomach. Ingo was my best friend, but seeing his never-ending good fortune . . . it drove me mad."

The Ramon in the truck stretches out his empty fingers, then makes a fist, as if he wishes he had a coin to grip too.

The truck rumbles away, carrying Ingo and Ramon down the road, away from us. I stare after it until the dust stings my eyes. When I peer back at Ramon's projection, his eyes are distant. And when he speaks, there is a low note of sadness that tightens my chest.

"So when I got the orders that I was going out on a scouting mission the next day and Ingo wasn't, I did what any person who wants to survive must do," he said. "I waited until lights-out, until Ingo snored and drool dribbled out of the side of his mouth. I slipped the anting-anting from his neck. I left for my scouting mission before the sun rose."

TEN

A **WHISTLE SHRIEKS. "HEY, FREDDIE, PAY ATTENTION!"** Mrs. Barnes yells from the sidelines.

Ramon's World War II world flickers and fades out, like an old-timey movie reaching the end of its film.

Mrs. Barnes holds her hand up to shield her brow from the sun, and she's squinting right at me. My team has moved halfway down the field. I sprint to catch up.

"I can't believe you stole it!" I growl through a jaw so tight my teeth might crack.

Ramon hid this key piece of information from me this whole time. *He* is the reason the evil spirits turned their viciousness in my family's direction in the first place. His one misdeed haunted our family for generations.

"Mom, Dad, Apong Rosing, and, heck, every person at Holy Redeemer Academy has drilled this into us: *Thou shalt not steal!*" I tuck the amulet back into my shirt as I near the rest of my team.

"I was scared!" Ramon snaps back. "I was only going to borrow it for my one mission. Ingo couldn't have known it was me. He must have cursed it after he realized it was gone."

I let out a frustrated growl, only to make unwelcome eye contact with the other team's goalkeeper, Molly, nearby. Her brown eyes quickly bounce back to the field, though. She was also at my failed soccer team tryout last year. She obviously doesn't see me as a scoring threat.

"Wait, if Ingo's the one who cursed it, maybe he can lift it," I say, my brain cells connecting dots faster than the soccer ball flying around the field. "Did you ask him about the bad luck when you tried to give the amulet back?"

Ramon rubs the back of his neck. "I never got a chance. While I was out on my mission, the Filipino and American forces at Bataan surrendered. By the time my team returned to the base, we were already preparing to march to a camp over sixty miles away."

"Was Ingo there too? On the march?"

He nods. "But the spirits were much angrier with me than they are with you. They seemed to find every possible way to keep me from Ingo. I could barely keep up on the march. Yes, I was one of the younger, healthier ones, but I had cut my hand badly on the day of the ninth notch. It got infected." He inspects his hand, as if he could see the wound still on it.

"And whenever I rallied enough energy to move closer to Ingo, the enemy soldiers stopped me and pushed me back into line." He sighs and drops his hand to his side. "I never did make it to that camp. I never did speak to my best friend again." The last of Ramon's words come out quietly.

Despite how much I want to stay mad, the rest of my anger fizzles out. While I was putting together my family tree board, Apong Rosing told me about the Bataan Death March as I scrawled down the names of her family. After the surrender to the Imperial Japanese forces, her brother and thousands of other soldiers were forced to march over sixty-five miles to crowded trains and ultimately prison camps.

It had seemed like such a faraway thing when she spoke of it. But now, seeing how it affected Ramon, I realize that the scars of war can last long after treaties and handshakes.

How can I be angry at him? He was scared. He must have seen things during the war that I can't even imagine now. He was just searching for something safe to cling to. Isn't that what I hoped for when I found the amulet in the first place?

Both of us had been so willing to believe that something —anything—could change our luck. But no anting-anting could have spared Ramon from an international war. No anting-anting could have kept him alive without food, water, and rest. No anting-anting would have diverted the gazes of the watchful enemy soldiers so he and Ingo could maybe, just maybe, escape into the jungle and to safety.

Ramon drags a hand through his hair. The strands fall back flat, unbothered by the breeze that's ruffling my own hair.

"I collapsed during the march," he says. "The last thing I saw was the spirit—one that looked just like me—at the edge of the road. When I opened my eyes again, I was in this amulet, staring out of an envelope and at Rosita. Someone must've found the anting-anting along with my dog tags and mailed me to her."

"And you couldn't speak to her until I reactivated the amulet at Tuesday Mass," I say.

His silence cuts right into me. Theses decades have been lonely for him. No one to talk to, to laugh with. As annoying as the Ruiz family curse has been for me, my bruises and minor moments of embarrassment are nothing compared to what Ramon has gone through. The curse isolates me from everyone, too, but at least I'm not trapped in a coin. The spirits punished him worst of all.

And now I, with this amulet in my hands, am the only one who can bring peace to any of us.

I'm about to press him for answers when a wisp of a shadow darkens the lower edge of my line of sight. A leg, I think, but none of my teammates are around. A scream of "Heads up!" cuts from across the field.

Then stars explode in my vision.

When the blackness fades, I'm flat on the ground, facing the bright blue sky. A dull pain thuds on both the back and front of my head.

A second later, the ground thunders around me. Faces appear, hovering above. Some look worried, but the rest of them—okay, most of them—seem to be holding back laughter.

I prop myself up on my elbows. The offending soccer ball sits guiltily to my right. Ramon's projection is nowhere to be found.

Now the whole class surrounds me, their loose jerseys flapping in the wind. I want to jump up and dash away from everyone's judging eyes, but those bright spots in my vision probably mean I should stay down for a minute longer. Meanwhile, laughter starts to spill out of my classmates' mouths.

"Back up, kids!" Mrs. Barnes, glowering, shoves her way through the wall of snickering students. She reaches out to help me up. "Let's get you to the nurse's office, Ruiz."

I grab her hand and haul myself up. I'm sure my face is tomato red as I brush the bits of grass off my butt.

More giggling. The entire seventh-grade class is going to hear about this by lunchtime. Then the whole school will know by the end of the day. As I trudge toward the sidelines, I can't decide what's worse: the laughter at my back, chasing me off the field, or the terrible thought that this is only the beginning of a getting-worse curse.

When I feel for the amulet in my pocket, the two notches on the coin remind me the clock is ticking.

The blow to my heart is ten times worse than a smack in the head with an underinflated soccer ball.

ELEVEN

FACEPLANT *FREDDIE COMMENTS FOLLOW ME ALL DAY.* Sharkey even hides her face behind her binder when she gets into Dad's truck with me after school. To be honest, my coolness level at school suffered more damage than my head did. Not that it was high to begin with. But with how Mom's fussing over my physical well-being, you'd think I was tackled by some hulking NFL linebacker.

She analyzes me over a glistening mound of spaghetti.

"How are you feeling?" she asks for the fourth time this hour. She's wearing an oversize, faded blue shirt with a cartoon character on it, which makes it a little hard for me to take her seriously.

"Fine. Same as I was when you asked me five minutes ago."

Dad and Mom exchange a look, the kind that means

they're going to gang up on me. I brace myself for the two-front attack.

"The school nurse said to watch out for any symptoms of a concussion," Dad says. "Do you have a headache? Neck pain?"

I shake my head.

It's probably for the best that I didn't get on the Holy Redeemer soccer team. I couldn't have handled this intense interrogation every time I showed up at home with an injury.

Mom and Dad always used to push this or that activity at me because they thought it odd that I'd rather spend all day at home, focused on my Robo-Warrior cards. But I preferred to play it safe rather than test the curse at the community pool or out at a golf course. Eventually they shrugged and left me alone. I think they consider it a win that I'm at least not out breaking windows or stealing old ladies' purses or something.

Mom's gaze lowers to the amulet on my chest. "What's that around your neck?"

"Oh, this?" I force a cheerful-sounding chuckle. I meant to tuck the amulet into my shirt when I changed out of my school uniform. But I couldn't avoid the mirror on the way out of my room, and that red bump on my head sure was distracting. I try to keep my voice casual. "I found it in the garage. I just thought the coin looked cool."

Apong Rosing sits up. At Ramon's request, I haven't shared what I learned about him and the anting-anting with her yet, to keep her safe from the spirits. She's been locked in a cycle of teleserye episodes, long phone calls with Grandma Nita, and planned and unplanned naps all afternoon anyway.

Apong clears her throat with a cough. "It's not only a coin. It's an anting-anting, like I told you yesterday."

I resist the urge to kick her under the table. I'm pretty sure you're not allowed to bump your great-grandmother's shin, even if she utterly betrays you. Apong continues hacking at her meatball, because she sees nothing weird about her great-grandson donning an amulet inhabited by her long-dead brother. I'm certain my parents won't feel the same way.

Mom frowns and sets down her fork. "Anting-anting? Freddie, you don't believe in that, do you?"

I try to look away, but with the four of us around a circular dining table, my gaze is bound to land on someone. So I focus on the next meatball and mumble a noncommittal "Iunno."

"It's just an old coin on a string." Mom presses on. "There's nothing magical about it." She's always hated the good luck charms I tried to sneak by her over the years. She owns a landfill's worth of confiscated four-leaf clovers, horseshoes, pennies I've picked up off the floor, and every other charm I've hoarded.

I move the meatball around my plate. My silence makes Mom bolder.

She picks up her fork and wags it at me like a gavel. "In fact, I'd prefer you not wear that. I'm sure it's against the school dress code."

I stuff a bite of meatball into my mouth to shove back the "but, Mom!" whine that's sure to make this worse. This conversation about a magical charm is actually going about as well as I could've hoped for. At least no one's yelling.

Dad, his eyebrows furrowed, angles to face Apong Rosing. "Apong, you can't be filling Freddie's head with this kind of nonsense."

Apong lifts her chin. "It's not nonsense."

I panic. She's not going to tell them about Ramon and our mission, is she? That's a surefire way to get the amulet taken away. As grating as Ramon is, I have no clue how I'll break this curse without his help.

Dad shakes his head. "It is nonsense. Just like there aren't duwende living under the calamansi tree in the backyard. And going to sleep with your hair wet doesn't make you blind."

Apong Rosing sniffs. "So what if you don't believe me? That doesn't make it untrue." She pounds a bony fist on the table in emphasis, then says to me, "And there are duwende at that tree, Freddie. Don't pick the calamansi without asking their permission first."

Thankfully, she's left out the mention of her ghost brother, but her words only deepen Dad's frown.

Mom shoots a look at me. "You've made Apong upset."

"What?" I lean back in my chair. "I'm not the one who upset her. I'm the only one at this table who believes her."

I know by that long look between Mom and Dad that I said the wrong thing.

Mom sighs. "He sounds confused."

"Maybe he does have a concussion," says my dad with zero medical training.

Their words pound in my ears, but it's not because I have a concussion (I think). "*He?* I'm right here!"

"Freddie," Dad says in that low warning tone, "calm down."

Which is exactly what not to say when you want someone angry to calm down.

I raise my voice. "And this isn't nonsense. This anting-anting is real. The family curse is real!" I cast a glance at Apong, who nods in a nonverbal "I told you so" to my parents.

For as long as I can remember, whenever Apong has brought up stories and beliefs rooted in Filipino magic and folklore that my parents don't understand—or don't want to understand—they dismiss it. If I can get them to listen to us now and to finally believe in everything Apong's been saying all these years, then we can break the curse together.

But before I can try to convince them, Apong butts in. There's a saying about catching more flies with honey than vinegar. Apong's way of convincing people is the verbal equivalent of dumping gallons of vinegar on them, like they do to football coaches with Gatorade after big wins.

"And what about Ritchie?" Apong snipes at my parents. "He believes in what you call 'nonsense.' It was this 'nonsense' that kept him alive."

Uncle Ritchie was born as baby Miguel, two months early. My Grandpa Carlo and his first wife, Grandma Irma, had worried that he wouldn't survive. Call him something else, Apong Rosing had suggested to them: it will confuse the spirits. And so they started calling baby Miguel Ritchie, after Ritchie Valens, the singer of one of Grandpa's favorite songs. Baby Ritchie quickly grew healthy and strong, they said, because the evil spirits were busy looking for a baby named Miguel. Now Uncle Ritchie's always the first to defend Apong Rosing and her ways.

Unfortunately, Dad never bought into that version of the tale. He shakes his head. "Right. As if modern medicine had nothing to do with it."

Apong Rosing huffs at Dad's sarcasm.

"Don't pretend like you don't remember him spending two thousand dollars on that shaman who was supposed to drive a ghost out of his apartment." Dad swivels his annoyed gaze to me. "He stayed in your room for two months, don't you remember?"

Suddenly the meatball goes sour in my mouth. I remember Uncle Ritchie's "visit." There wasn't a ghost in his apartment —the hissing was from the water heater—but of course that con artist took my uncle's money anyway. Which meant that Uncle Ritchie ultimately couldn't make rent, so he bunked with us at the beginning of last school year. More specifically, he carved out a corner of my room to lay down some blankets and a suitcase of his stuff. He still has a couple shirts hanging in my closet.

"I get that you don't want to see me go down that route, but we can't ignore this curse, Dad."

"And why not?" Mom cuts in.

I pause. I need my parents to take me and the curse seriously. But hearing how they speak of Uncle Ritchie, even a year later, doesn't give me much confidence about how they'll react.

My situation is different than my uncle's. Ramon is a real, non-water-heater-related ghost, not that my nonbelieving parents can see him, and this amped-up curse puts me in actual danger. My parents are already worried about whether

I have a brain injury from that spirit-guided soccer ball. This is my chance to spin that worry into curse-breaking action.

If I can get them to believe me.

I square my shoulders. "Because the curse is going to kill me."

Apong gasps, and she glares at the amulet like she's blaming Ramon for not telling her.

Dad shakes his head. "Wait, what? Who's going to kill you?"

"The curse's spirits!" I bang a fist on the table like Apong did. "You have to believe me. I woke the anting-anting, and now these spirits are—"

Dad stands up so quickly he nearly knocks his plate of spaghetti over. "That's it. I've had enough of this kind of talk. That coin isn't magical, and evil spirits aren't going to kill you. *We* don't believe in those things in this house."

He lifts his chin in defiance as he speaks. But I don't know how he can defy something that runs in his family's blood. Heritage doesn't disappear just because you change location. Forces can still affect you even if you don't believe in them.

With her tight jaw, Mom looks equally fed up. "We don't want to hear another word of this anting-anting business again," she says as she sticks her hand out.

My fingers instinctively fly to protect the amulet on my

chest. Mom wants to take it away. But without it, my life will be over in ten days.

"Hand it over, Freddie."

My hands shaking, I lift the amulet up and over my head. I tried to reason with them, to make them see that I need their help. And it backfired. In fact, now they seem even more dead set against the whole idea that this kind of magic exists.

I pause, my brain snagging on that last thought. "Fine, I won't ever mention it. But since you think this is just some silly old coin anyway, there's no harm in me keeping it, right?"

"It's a precious family heirloom. Freddie should hold on to it," Apong says, with a sympathetic glint in her eye when she looks at me. "I would not want it getting lost or discarded in the garage somewhere."

My parents' eyes flare when they realize that not only has their anti-magic argument been turned against them, but now they look like the bad guys for storing something important to Apong in a rusty drawer all these years.

Dad plops back into his seat. "Just put it away, then, and let's finish our dinner in peace. Our spaghetti's getting cold."

I slip the amulet into my pocket and pick up my fork. A small truce, but it hits me like a huge defeat. Now I know for certain I can't bring up the curse to them ever again. They'll take away the amulet. The fact that I can't count on them hurts my feelings (and my chances at survival).

Dad gives an approving nod once the amulet is out of sight and turns his attention back to his plate. Apong Rosing mumbles to herself—or to Ramon—in Ilocano, and I concentrate on shoveling down the rest of my spaghetti.

I'm disappointed this conversation didn't end in the grand "we'll help you save the day!" gesture I'd hoped for, but at least it's over. The sooner Mom and Dad forget about the anting-anting, the better. I already have evil spirits trying to keep me from breaking the curse: I don't need my parents in the mix too.

TWELVE

*T*WO DAYS AFTER THAT DISASTER OF A SPAGHETTI DINNER, Sharkey and I speed walk to the school library after our last class to make sure we get spaces at the computers. Competition for these screens is fierce. If you ever want to see gladiator-level fight action, put six computers in front of a dozen cell-phone-free kids whose parents are picking them up late on a Friday.

I plop in front of the clunky computer farthest from Ms. Perez, the tough librarian with the powerful shush. She flits her eyes up at me briefly, just enough to impart that "I'm watching you, kid" threat, then goes back to reading whatever's on her desk. I accidentally spilled a water bottle all over the carefully arranged NEW BOOKS! display a few months ago, and she hasn't forgiven or forgotten.

Her quick glance is enough to make me consider moving,

but kids are already snatching up the other desktops like it's musical chairs.

I log in to one computer, and Sharkey grabs the other. She sets her science textbook between us and opens it up to a random page—a nice prop to cover up what we're really doing. To Ms. Perez, we'll look like we're studying mitosis together, not chasing down an old man to break a curse. At least these school computers aren't Dad-monitored and time-controlled like my one at home.

Ramon projects himself out next to us, seating himself on the desk. He swings his legs as our computers process our login info. He squints at the bulletin board. "Robo-Warrior Competition, Junior League, ages ten through twelve," he reads. "Robo-Warrior? What is the meaning of this?"

Before answering, I look around to make sure no one's lurking nearby. "Only the coolest card game out there. You collect Robo-Warrior cards and use them to battle other kids."

Ramon blinks. "So you throw these cards at the other children?"

Sharkey chuckles. "No, no. You don't throw them."

"Then how do you battle? Weaponless, you will lose."

Sharkey smacks a palm to her forehead. "The cards represent different attacks, boosts, abilities, and stuff." She juts a thumb at me. "Freddie here is great at the game."

Ramon's eyebrows rise. He seems impressed, even if playing Robo-Warrior doesn't actually mean hurling cardboard rectangles at other people.

I sit up a little taller. "It's one of the few things I can actually compete in without worrying about getting beaned by a ball or puck or cleat."

Sharkey nods. "It's true. We can't all be the smoothest break-dancers in our age group in the Southwestern region. And our performance at the Spring Showcase is going to prove it." She inspects her nails in an obviously fake show of humility.

"You should compete in this card tournament, Freddie," Ramon says. "It's in two weeks."

I gulp. "If I'm alive in two weeks."

I shift in my chair, the reminder of my impending doom making me uneasy. "It's been four days since I woke up those evil spirits, and I've got the four notches on this amulet to prove it. Let's hurry up and find Ingo," I whisper, pulling up a search browser. "He's the one who cursed the amulet, so he must be able to uncurse it, too."

I type in "Ingo Agustin" and send a silent prayer up into the universe for something, anything, helpful as I hit the Enter key. But none of the results on the first page even look remotely relevant.

Sharkey leans toward the screen and sweeps the bangs

out of her eyes. "All these results are for young people!" She peers at Ramon. "No offense."

Ramon shrugs. "None taken."

"Maybe some of these are your friend's relatives," I offer. Names could run in families. I, for example, was named after Mom's father, Alfredo. Or after the delicious Italian dish. Both good.

I click on the first search result, but Ramon's groan signals it's not the right Agustin family.

"No, no, no," Ramon says, shaking his head with each word. "Ingo's eyes were smaller, more set apart. This boy looks like those Kit-Cat Klocks." Ramon laughs at his own joke, but Sharkey and I just blink at each other.

"You know, the ones whose eyes move?" Ramon urges. He widens his eyes and swings his gaze back and forth. Left, right, left, right. "Like this?"

"Any idea what he's talking about?" Sharkey whispers out the side of her mouth.

"No clue."

"Hey!" Ramon cuts in. "I'm right here. It's disrespectful to talk about me, your elder, like that. Don't they teach you any manners these days?"

Sharkey groans, and I suppress a laugh. Like his sister, Ramon seems to have a whole lot of opinions about what people should be teaching us.

I click on the next result, then the next one, but no luck. I know it's unlikely we are going to find anything online about a man almost a century old, half a world away. Still, part of me hopes that maybe there's a bread crumb somewhere. Page after page of search results crush my dreams quickly.

Sharkey slides her hand off the mouse. "This is going nowhere, Freddie."

"Well, do you two have any ideas?" I ask, folding my arms across my chest. "I'm the one who got hit in the head with a soccer ball yesterday. I can't be doing all the heavy thinking here."

The memory of last night's concussion-centered dinner floats back to me, and something strikes like a match in my head: Dad's warning about Uncle Ritchie. The warning itself isn't important, but another part of the story is. Uncle Ritchie isn't really a Ritchie.

I glance up at my cousin, the idea kicking into a full-blown revelation. Sharkey isn't really a Sharkey either.

Ritchie and Sharkey are nicknames.

"Maybe Ingo is a nickname," I say.

I practically see the lightbulb switch on above Ramon's head. "Why didn't I think of that? You are smarter than you look, Freddie."

"Um, thanks?"

Ramon's face twists in deep thought. "I don't recall his full name. I only ever called him Ingo. Even his brothers called him that."

Sharkey straightens in her chair. "The nickname might be related to his real name, like how Mike is short for Michael!"

Or—and I really hope this isn't the case—it could be a nickname plucked out of thin air, like Ritchie for Miguel.

Sharkey crisscrosses her legs underneath her on the hard wooden chair. She clacks away at the keyboard. In seconds, she pulls up a list of possible names Ingo could be short for.

"Huh," she says, her head bobbing to a beat playing only in her head. "Turns out Ingo's a full name on its own. Could be German, Scandinavian, or even French."

Ramon slides off the desk. "I do not think the Agustins had strong German, Scandinavian, or French ties. If anything, his first name may have Spanish roots. And we tried looking for a plain Ingo Agustin already, did we not? And we found nothing?"

Sharkey shoots him an impatient look. "You say 'we' like you're actually doing the grunt work yourself. But no, we didn't find anything. I'll keep looking."

I stifle a grin. Watching Sharkey argue with a projection is amusing. I'm glad I'm not the only one who finds my great-granduncle a little irritating.

I finish typing in my own search terms and hit the Enter key. But instead of the search results flashing onto the screen, the whole monitor fizzles and there's a loud pop. I find myself staring at my slack-jawed, wide-eyed self in the black screen.

Great. I've broken the school computer. I even spy a hint of smoke wafting from the desktop tower.

As if she has a sixth sense for school property, Ms. Perez calls over, "What's going on there, Freddie?"

Lightning-fast, Sharkey clicks to another browser tab— one that has diagrams of cells.

I scoot my chair back, scrunching up my shoulders in an I-have-no-clue gesture.

Ms. Perez sighs loudly and shuffles over. She pokes at the power buttons on the monitor and the desktop tower. Nothing.

Ms. Perez sighs again—more frustrated than angry this time—and unplugs the keyboard and mouse. She hands them to me. "Here, help me bring this to the storage room, will you? These things are a decade old. Maybe the administrators will finally buy us new ones."

I grab the equipment and follow her. A quick glance behind me confirms that Sharkey's already switched back to her original browser tab. She mumbles something to Ramon.

At least those two can continue the search, thanks to my accidental luring away of Ms. Perez.

On the way back to the library, I spot a grimy penny, kicked to the side of the hallway. I dust it off before I pocket it.

"For good luck?" Ms. Perez asks.

I scan her face for sarcasm. After all those warnings from Mom and Dad, I don't have a lot of faith in adults understanding what I'm trying to do. But Ms. Perez looks sincere. I offer a simple "Yup."

"Find a penny, pick it up. All day long, you'll have good luck," she says in a singsong voice.

I can't help the small smile that creeps onto my face. It's nice to run into someone who doesn't dismiss all my bad luck talk right away (or make fun of me for it).

When I finally return to the library, I can tell from Sharkey's grin that she has happy news. It's a good thing I picked up that penny.

She leaps up from her chair. "Domingo. His name is Domingo! Ramon finally remembered!" Excitement crackles through her whisper.

Projecting next to me, Ramon nods in agreement. "And Sharkey has written down telephone numbers we can try."

If we weren't in the school library, I would've let out a

whoop at this slight win. No way I'm going to try Ms. Perez's patience after wrecking that computer, though.

"Now we just have to start calling these possible Domingo Agustins. Are they all in the Philippines?" I ask. My parents would notice if our phone bill included hundreds of dollars in international calls. And by notice, I mean blow up and ground me forever.

Sharkey shakes her head. "There are over a dozen Domingo Agustins scattered all around the world, and there's a couple here in the US, too. I'll show you." She whips back to the desk to rip out a page from her notebook.

I see it more clearly this time, a blurry shadow in the shape of a hand, its ghastly white fingers outstretched so it looks more like a claw.

A puzzle clicks together in my brain: this shadow has been following me ever since I activated the amulet.

This can't be good at all.

One look at the sudden fear in Ramon's eyes confirms it. He senses spirits nearby too.

The curse is about to get worse.

I open my mouth to shout a warning to Sharkey as she swivels to show me her notes. And that's when she, hands down the most coordinated kid I've ever known, trips over her own foot.

She goes down in slow motion. Her bangs fly up, revealing

too-round panicked eyes. A shrill wail escapes her lips. Her hands flail for something to catch her and they seize, to my horror, my pant leg.

Sharkey lands with a graceless thump on the ground. The torn notebook page is crushed under her hand. Inches away, a frayed power cord sizzles, but Sharkey yanks the notebook page away just in time to avoid a spark.

And around my ankles are my blue uniform pants, with my Elmo boxers on display for the whole library to see. My whole face flushes to match the glaring shade of *Sesame-Street*-puppet red.

The once-silent library erupts in laughter. I hadn't even realized there were that many kids in here.

"They were on sale!" I blurt out, as if that would help. I stopped watching *Sesame Street* years ago, but Mom bought a ten-pack on clearance. And as Dad said earlier this week when my pen exploded, cloth is cloth. Which reminds me this is the second time in a matter of days that kids at school have seen me in a situation involving underwear.

I'm spending way too much time thinking while the smiling Elmo on my butt is still on full display.

I swoop down to pull up my pants and help Sharkey, but she ignores me. Her hands, one still holding the ripped paper, go to her ankle. She drags in a sharp breath through her clenched teeth.

Suddenly my fallen pants and Elmo butt seem like the least of our problems. The curse's spirits can affect non-Ruizes too.

Ms. Perez, fastest librarian alive, is over to us in a second. "Sharlene, are you all right?"

Sharkey shakes her head, the tears already collecting on the rims of her eyes. "I—I can't get up!"

FOURTEEN
~~THIRTEEN~~

TOO UNLUCKY!

"*H*OLD STILL," APONG ROSING WARNS.

Sharkey squirms one more time but then settles down into the dining chair. It's hard to tell what her grimace is from: her sprained ankle or having Apong's home remedies inflicted on her.

Sharkey's got one leg propped up on one of our dining chairs. Apong Rosing, still in her purple dialysis cardigan, vultures over it, stacking warm ginger on Sharkey's ankle like it's a layer cake. A nearby roll of gauze will hold it all together.

After Sharkey tripped, the school nurse came and checked out her sprain. He pursed his mustache-topped lips at me as if he knew I had something to do with it, since I'd been in his office just yesterday.

Then we'd called her parents, who swore they'd be home

as soon as they could. Dad picked us up, and we called her aunt, a doctor across town, who gave us specific instructions on how to care for Sharkey's sprain at home. Now it's Apong Rosing's turn.

From my spot by the stove, the smell of charred ginger tickles my nose. Apong had sliced up almost a whole knob of it and roasted the pieces over the open blue flame of the stove. The rest of the root sits on the counter. It'll probably make its way into tonight's dinner somehow. Apong Rosing doesn't waste food.

While Sharkey is stuck under Apong's care, I stand here as moral support and as an extra pair of hands, in case Apong needs a scalpel or wrench or whatever else her home remedy requires. I can't think of anything else to do to be helpful. Sharkey's hurt because of me and my curse.

Sharkey eyes the swollen ankle disappearing beneath uneven ginger slices. "Um, I can just wait until my parents get here."

Apong gives a dismissive grunt and doesn't stop working. "The sooner we treat this, the better."

"But my aunt said to minimize swelling, not . . ." She waves a hand at her ankle. "Marinate it."

I disguise my laugh with a cough. I swear I've seen Apong apply this same ginger-layering technique to a hunk of pork, but Sharkey wouldn't want to hear that.

Apong reaches for another handful of ginger slices. "This ginger will help with the swelling. Now stop moving around so I can finish!"

Sharkey's wary eyes shift to me, and I shrug. We can look it up online later, but I'm not about to second-guess Apong right in front of her. I scrunch my face and wave a hand in front of my nose. "Too bad the ginger won't minimize its own smell, too."

Sharkey's gaze turns murderous. It's a good thing Apong's got her stuck in that chair.

Apong Rosing secures the bandage and leans away, her hands on her lower back. She gives a satisfied nod. "There. All done. You rest here. Are you hungry?"

I think of the leftover gingerroot on the counter and mouth a "no" at Sharkey. We might both leak ginger smell out of our pores for days, if Apong has her way.

Sharkey shakes her head and manages a polite smile. "No, thank you. It's already almost four o'clock, and I wouldn't want to ruin my dinner."

"Such a good girl," Apong says with a smile.

I roll my eyes and pull out the amulet. "Ramon," I whisper. Engraved in the coin, his face turns to me. "Do you think it's okay if we ask Apong Rosing for her cell phone and calling card?"

Before he can answer, Apong huffs. "Why are you asking my brother? I am sitting right here."

"The curse's spirits," Sharkey explains. "If you help Freddie, they might try to hurt you too." Her eyes drift toward her ankle then, and she frowns.

I wonder if she regrets helping me. Now everyone has *more* of a reason not to hang out with me.

"It's true." I lower my eyes to the floor. "The spirits aren't just trying to hurt me. They're hurting anyone who's helping me. They caused Sharkey's fall, I know it. I've seen these shadows every time something awful has happened."

Ramon shakes his head. "Yes, those are the evil spirits that carry out the curse, Freddie. I warned you that they would be out for blood, did I not? I was foolish to believe they wouldn't harm others to keep the curse going. Sharkey's injury could have been much worse if her reflexes were as poor as yours."

Apong dismisses our concerns with a wave. "Oh, please. I am a Ruiz. I am just as cursed as you, and I still survived wars, plagues, and birthing your Grandpa Carlo—the biggest baby boy the midwife had ever seen—without medication. I can handle a few spirits."

In the coin, Ramon keeps shaking his head. "No, no, no. Rosita, this is different. See what they did to Sharkey? As your older brother, I cannot let harm come to you."

"What are you going to do? Jump out of that anting-anting and twist my arm? You didn't even tell me how much danger Freddie is in! I must help."

Ramon's face goes tight with annoyance. I'm sure he's made this face at his little sister a thousand times. "Rosita, it is much too risky for you to get involved. You must listen to me! You must respect your manong."

Apong Rosing narrows her eyes as we all try to calculate whether she's going to buy Ramon's respect-your-elders argument. Sure, he's technically older, but he also looks like a seventeen-year-old and, well, she doesn't. She also spent the majority of her life not having to listen to a brother, thanks to the curse. After a moment, Apong grumbles under her breath, like she does when she's angry at Dad. Ramon seems to understand what she says, though, because his coin face relaxes.

"Good," he says, shifting his gaze to me. "I do not sense the spirits around. Perhaps a few telephone calls to find Ingo will be safe, if Rosita stays out of it."

Apong Rosing braces both ginger-scented hands on the wooden dining chair arms and begins her slow rise. "But before you waste my calling card minutes, why don't you try your Uncle Ritchie first? He's in the Philippines for business all month. He's supposed to drop by Santa Maria for a few days to visit your Grandma Nita."

"Rosita, helping Freddie—"

Apong cuts her brother off with a wave. "I'm simply telling him about his uncle's schedule. Surely the spirits will see nothing wrong with that."

I can't help but smile at Apong's courage, even against her brother's wishes. Excitement bubbles up in my stomach at what she'd said. If Uncle Ritchie's in Santa Maria, he could ask around town in person. Someone's got to know where Ingo Agustin went.

"Rosita!" Ramon says. "I told you it is too risky for you to help!"

"And you said there were no spirits around!"

It's Ramon's turn to narrow his eyes, and they glare at each other like it's some Wild West cowboy standoff. I can't believe I was ever jealous of their sibling bond.

"Get my phone and the card, Freddie. You know where it is." Apong stretches her back and grunts as one of her joints cracks. "And tell Ritchie to make sure he gave that box of chocolate to Nita. He'd better not have eaten it himself."

I dash off to Apong's room before she can change her mind or before she and Ramon find something else to bicker about. The unlucky penny from the school hallway clinks against the pen in my pocket.

I round the corner fast, and the amulet thunks against my chest.

"Slow down!" Ramon snaps. "I'm going to throw up in here."

I smooth out my run and glide into Apong's room. I head straight for the hot-pink plastic bin on her desk. That's where she keeps all the fancy electronics she owns: the cell phone Dad bought her, the old iPad she uses to play sudoku, and charging cords that I'm not sure belong to anything. I pocket the cell phone and slide the bright red phone card off the Danish butter cookie tin Apong uses to store her sewing supplies.

I'm on my way out the door when Ramon stops me with a "Wait! What's that?"

I pause. It takes me a moment to realize that Ramon has spotted the family picture on Apong Rosing's dresser. I take a couple steps toward it, but I make no move to pick it up. She'll know if I touch it. She always does, just like she always knows when I take one of the cookies out of her blue tins before they become needle and thread storage.

Ramon goes quiet. He projects himself out of the amulet and stands there, his gaze on the photograph. His fingers drift toward it, but they go straight through. His frown deepens.

I don't have anything to say that could help with whatever painful memories he must be facing. I can't even leave the room to give him a brief moment of privacy: the amulet hangs from a solid leather string around my neck.

"That's what I used to look like," Ramon says, his voice distant.

I peer at his face, frozen in time, in the family portrait. "You look the same." Same hair, same posture, same sense of smugness. He's been the same for decades because of that curse.

"I wonder what I would've looked like as an old man."

There's a sadness to his words that makes my chest tighten. He doesn't come off annoying anymore. Just heartbroken.

I try to bring some lightness back into everything. "Well, judging by the genes Apong Rosing passed down from your family, you probably wouldn't have grown any taller. Or had a lot of hair on your head. And you would've looked weird with a beard."

Ramon chuckles softly and then goes silent again. After a while, he lets out a long sigh. "You are a good friend, Freddie. Like Ingo, always trying to make me laugh. Now, let's go start these telephone calls. We need to break this curse so that I can go free and you can live many decades bald, with a weird beard."

I stroll back toward the kitchen, and for the first time, I don't really mind Ramon walking next to me.

FIFTEEN

"I'M SORRY, THE NUMBER YOU HAVE DIALED IS NO LONGER in service."

My shoulders slump at the sound of the prerecorded message.

"What does this mean? Did you dial correctly?" Ramon asks, his eyebrows furrowed.

Sharkey reaches across the kitchen table for the phone in my hand. "Let me try."

"I dialed the right number, see?" I flash the screen at her and Ramon so they can compare it to what's listed in Apong Rosing's ragged address book. "How are we supposed to reach him if his cell's not working?"

"There are other ways to communicate than a mobile phone," Apong says with a snort, from the kitchen counter.

She's juggling a chayote squash, an onion, and an easily shatterable bottle of fish sauce. "You children always think the more technology, the better."

I open my mouth to reply, but Ramon beats me to it.

"So what would you suggest, Rosita?" We must still be spirit-free if he's feeling at ease enough to ask her this small question.

Apong dumps the produce and fish sauce on the counter. "Try Nita's house number." She points at the address book with a pucker of her lips.

I flip open Apong's address book to the right page and start dialing. Sharkey and Ramon cross their fingers.

The line rings and crackles before a woman's voice comes on. "Hello?"

I scoot to the edge of the dining chair. Before I can answer, Apong shoves her way closer to the phone (even though we're on speaker mode, and she could've yelled from across the kitchen). "Nita, is Ritchie there? Did he give you the chocolates I sent?"

"Auntie Rosing! Yes, Ritchie is here. Salamat po for the chocolate. One moment," Grandma Nita says before shrieking my uncle's name (thankfully away from the phone's receiver).

"Hi, Grandma," Uncle Ritchie says, his voice hoarse, like he just woke up. "We're getting ready to eat breakfast."

"You were supposed to call me when you got there!" Apong snaps. "So I know you're safe!"

A snicker, then, "Well, here I am, safe." There's a smile in his words. He's used to this kind of pushy care from her. We all are. "I left my work bag in a jeepney a couple of days ago, with my laptop and cell phone in it. Had to disconnect it all and freeze my accounts, and now my business partners are annoyed they can't reach me either."

Ramon and I exchange a glance. The work bag incident could've been Uncle Ritchie's fault, but I'm willing to bet the curse had something to do with it too.

"And I should've gotten here yesterday afternoon, but the bus broke down," my uncle continues. "I got here so late I just went straight to sleep."

The clang of pots and pans floats through the cell phone speaker, and I can imagine them all crowded in the kitchen together, just like we are. Except they must be surrounded by the sizzle and smell of Spam, fried fish, or eggs. Here, we're still living in the ginger cloud.

Apong Rosing backs off, satisfied that Uncle Ritchie got to Santa Maria in one piece. Then she goes to busy herself at the stove with the ginger she didn't plaster on Sharkey's ankle.

I inch closer to the phone, just in case Apong tries to physically butt back in. "Hi, Uncle Ritchie, Freddie here."

"And Sharkey!" she adds from the seat next to me.

"And Ramon!" he adds, from his projection next to Apong.

"Hi, Freddie, hi, Sharkey," my uncle replies.

Ramon deflates at the realization that talking on the phone isn't one of his projection powers. "It was worth a try," he mumbles.

I send him a sympathetic smile, then continue. "Uncle, we have a big favor to ask. Can you ask around for someone named Domingo Agustin? I need to find him right away. We're trying to break the family curse. It's a matter of life and death."

A long pause, during which my heart thumps a drum solo in my chest.

"Sorry, you cut out there, Fredster. The connection's a little wonky. What was that name again?"

I blow out a small sigh of relief. The delay wasn't Uncle Ritchie saying no or gearing up to lecture me about the curse. "Domingo Agustin. He used to live in Santa Maria. He's around Apong Rosing's age."

"And he's still alive?"

Apong slams a bowl on the counter. "You disrespectful —"

"Yes, he's still alive," Sharkey hurries in.

Over at the kitchen counter, Ramon focuses on calming

his sister down so she doesn't pelt a knob of ginger at the phone.

"Auntie Nita, have you heard of a Domingo Agustin?" Uncle Ritchie asks. Then there's some mumbled conversation we can't really hear, interrupted every few seconds by a weird crackle or buzz on the line.

"Why's it making that noise?" Sharkey asks.

"It's probably Apong's old phone. Or Grandma Nita's landline. Or the fact that Apong chose the calling card based on which teleserye star was in the commercial."

I tap my fingers on the table while we wait for Uncle Ritchie to investigate. I notice Sharkey's doing the same thing, but to that beat that plays in her head. Even with her ankle swollen to the size of a pandesal, she's mentally rehearsing for her dance crew's Spring Showcase.

"Rosita, you need to be more careful. That knife seems sharp," Ramon warns while we're waiting. He bites his lip, watching his sister hack away at the ginger.

Sharkey pauses her drumming and nudges the pair of thick, gold-rimmed glasses sitting next to her on the dining table. "And don't you need these things?"

Worry wriggles in my chest. "Apong, you probably should wait until my parents get home. They'll take care of dinner."

Apong Rosing snorts and continues chopping up ginger.

"They don't cook half as well as I do. They're always using canned this, powdered that. This"—she points at the ginger with her knife—"is fresh. Better for chicken tinola."

She then swings her knife at the pack of chicken thighs defrosting in the kitchen sink. First of all, a lady from a cursed family shouldn't be waving a sharp knife around like that. Second, I wonder if the curse's spirits are savvy enough to cultivate salmonella on that raw meat that's been sitting out all day.

"Besides," Apong says, returning to the ginger, "I'm not the one who angered these spirits. These spirits are mostly after you, Freddie. And as commanded"—she shoots a venomous glare at her brother—"I am not getting involved."

Her attempt at reassurance makes me feel both better and worse. I groan as Uncle Ritchie's tinny voice blares through the phone on the table. "Sorry for the wait, Fredster, but Auntie Nita went to ask her neighbor. It took a while because the guy's got old-timer's, and it's a bad day. She had to calm him down because he was confused and got angry at her."

The confusion must be plain on my own face because Apong Rosing cuts in softly. "Old-timer's: he means Alzheimer's disease. The neighbor might have trouble remembering some days."

I nod and focus back on Uncle Ritchie.

"Get this: the neighbor's nephew's best friend is married to Domingo's son!"

Sharkey bolts upright from her slouch. "Seriously? What are the odds?"

Uncle Ritchie laughs. "I know, right? And speaking of odds, guess where Domingo is!"

I lean forward, my hand tightening around my blue pen. Domingo exists, and someone somewhere knows where to find him!

"No guessing," Apong Rosing snaps. "You're using all my minutes."

"You're no fun, Grandma. According to Auntie Nita's neighbor, Domingo lives by his son and his family in—"

Crackle.

Then buzz.

Then silence.

"Uncle Ritchie?" My voice trembles. I lunge for Apong Rosing's cell phone and mash at the screen. But the call's been dropped. "You're kidding me! No no no!"

Sharkey shoves the calling card at me. "Call them again!"

My fingers fly across the buttons so fast that I get the calling card access code wrong twice. Then I'm met with the frustrating beep of a busy signal. Same sound on the second or third time I try to call, too. We can't even text them to call us because they're on an old landline phone.

Then a recorded message plays, telling us we're out of calling card minutes.

I kick the leg of the table.

Ramon projects next to me. "I told you. The spirits are not going to make it easy for us to get rid of them."

"Can you email your uncle? Or send him a Facebook message or something?" Sharkey asks.

I slouch. "Not anytime soon. Even if Dad unlocks the laptop for me right now, I can't have him peeking over my shoulder while we're writing to his brother about the curse. He'd make me delete it for sure." I glance over at Sharkey's house. "What about you?"

Sharkey shakes her head. "I accidentally left my tablet in my mom's car, and our computer's got time limits. I can only use it from five to seven p.m."

How do our parents even know how to do all this? I shouldn't have let them go to that last open house at school, when they had that tech expert doing demos and handing out brochures.

"Well, at least we know Ingo's alive, somewhere," Sharkey says, deflated.

I thump my head down onto the dining table. "This can't be happening. We're so close to finding him, I know it." Trying to break this curse is starting to feel like fighting to take two steps forward, only to get shoved one step back.

A bang on the glass sliding door makes all of us jump. Uncle Sammy, worry plastered across his face, motions at me to unlock the door. He still has his work badge hanging from his front pocket. His eyes are locked on Sharkey's ginger-wrapped limb.

Sharkey frowns at her dad and then at me. "Sorry, Freddie. We'll try again tomorrow, okay? We'll figure this out."

I unlock the door, and Uncle Sammy comes hurricaning in, demanding the who what when where of Sharkey's injury and treatment. Neither she nor Apong say a word about the curse, but I know it's on all of our minds. Those spirits are trying to cut me off from my allies: first Sharkey, and now Uncle Ritchie.

And without the slightest idea where Ingo is, I'm powerless to stop them.

SIXTEEN

*T*HE BLARE OF APONG ROSING'S TELEVISION SHOW REACHES
us all the way in my room, down the hall, with the door
closed. She's watching the teleserye episode she recorded yesterday. She had missed it to treat Sharkey's ankle and pester
Uncle Ritchie about the chocolate delivery. And this catch-
up is on top of her regular three-hour teleserye marathon on
Saturdays, all to keep up with her die-hard-fan friends at the
dialysis center.

The timing of this distraction actually works out in my
favor. First, I don't need Apong yelling over my shoulder to
every Domingo Agustin we call this afternoon. Second, she's
determined to help me break the curse, but Ramon is equally
determined to keep his little sister out of harm's way. I'd prefer to stay out of this sibling struggle, and the teleserye break
thankfully serves as a little time-out.

In my desk chair, because she still refuses to sit anywhere else in my "filthy" room, Sharkey taps away at a dance simulator on her tablet. The ginger lump around her ankle is gone, replaced with a neon-orange athletic wrap. It gave her a way out of Uncle Sammy's company picnic this afternoon. That means she's at our house for a few hours.

Mom's out, and Dad's been in the driveway with his truck all day, trying to figure out what's making that loud clang. So we've got perfect, parent-free conditions for the task ahead.

I sit on the floor next to Sharkey, pushing aside a juice-stained sweater that's been in that spot for two weeks. (Okay, maybe she has a point about my room being filthy.)

I position the amulet, Apong Rosing's new topped-up calling card, and her cell phone between us. I'm determined not to let yesterday's bad phone connection and zero-balance card get in the way of breaking this curse. "You got the phone number list?"

Sharkey pulls the crumpled piece of notebook paper from her backpack, and I spread it out in front of me on the carpet.

I scrunch my nose at the many Domingo Agustins and wide range of locations. "Where do we even start?"

Ramon projects next to me. "Go in alphabetical order."

I purse my lips in my best "are you serious?" look.

He somehow takes that as encouragement and laughs at his own joke. "Get it? Because they're all named Domingo Agustin! Funny, no?"

Sharkey and I exchange a bored glance.

"You children have no sense of humor," he says, crossing his arms.

"Too bad they don't teach it in schools these days," I say.

He huffs at my teasing. "You wouldn't last a moment in my elementary school, Freddie. You don't even sing. We used to sing every day. I had the best voice, of course. Listen—" He clears his throat with a cough and draws in a deep breath.

"Let's just go down the list, Sharkey," I blurt out, cutting off whatever melody he was about to belt out.

Ramon huffs again and mutters something about me being jealous.

Sharkey rolls her eyes at both of us, then reads the first phone number aloud. I put the cell phone on speaker mode and dial.

We all lean toward the phone as it rings.

All my nervousness from the past few days seems to have just piled up, a tower ready to topple at the slightest nudge. And I'm pushed with each call we make: the first person who answers isn't Domingo Agustin. Neither is the second. None of these Domingo Agustins in the Philippines seemed to be *the* Domingo Agustin.

A few sound much younger than ninety years old and, when asked, admit they didn't know anyone older with that name. Every time I hang up and Sharkey scratches a number off our list, my hopes that we've caught Ingo or one of his relatives fizzle.

"Well, that was a bust," Sharkey says the second the line goes dead on our fifth phone call. "Ready to try some of these US numbers?"

My legs are falling asleep from sitting in this position for so long. "We're never going to find this guy. With my luck, he lives in a cave or a submarine or some other unreachable place."

"We cannot give up," Ramon says. "Look what's already happened to you. And your uncle, and Sharkey's ankle."

Sharkey frowns. "He's right. We have to keep trying, bad luck or not."

I peer down at the list and all the inked-out numbers. There are still a few numbers left to call, a few numbers to be disappointed by. "Too bad Uncle Ritchie didn't give us more helpful info," I grumble.

Sharkey pauses for a moment. I can practically see the lightbulb that pops up in her head a second later. "Maybe he did! Think about what he said, Freddie." Her eyes scan the list.

I glance over, too, but I can't tell what Sharkey's searching for. "He didn't say anything, though. He got cut off."

"But before that, he said something about odds, remember? And what do you think of when you think of odds?"

I blink. "Math homework?"

She smacks a palm to her forehead. "No, gambling. I think Uncle Ritchie was trying, badly, to be funny. Which seems to run in your family." She casts a quick look at Ramon, then leans down and jabs a finger at one line on the paper. It lands on a string of numbers with *Nevada* scrawled next to it. "Nevada's got tons of casinos."

I'm hit then with the memory of our families' Las Vegas road trip last summer. Sharkey and I were dragged to so many outlet stores. Then the adults would stay up late at the poker tables and slot machines while we got stuck watching movies in the room with a snoring Apong Rosing.

"Dial this one," Sharkey says. "I've got a good feeling about it."

Nevada is a big state, but it's worth a try. Plus, the hope in her voice is contagious. But then my eyes land on her ankle wrap on their way down to the phone. I pause with my hand on the receiver. "Um, I can do this later."

Sharkey raises her eyebrow. "Are you joking? Why not now?"

I squirm, suddenly very uncomfortable. I angle and pluck a wadded-up sock from underneath my leg. "You've already done enough. I don't want to drag you through any more of this. If the spirits—"

"They've already got me. What are they going to do, sprain the other ankle?"

"Yeah, but—"

"But nothing. I said I'd help, didn't I?"

"But you don't have to!" I toss the sock at my laundry hamper and miss. "I'm the cursed one. You only got hurt because of me. The less time you spend with me, the safer you are."

She crosses her arms and glares down at me. "You're not the only one who's been affected by this curse all this time. How many times have I wanted to go to the pool or mini golfing or skating and my parents say, 'Only if Freddie goes'?"

I keep my mouth shut. I know where this is going. Ramon takes a cue from me and keeps his lips zipped, for once.

Sharkey gives a sharp nod. "That's right. A million times. And you never want to go because you're always so afraid of the curse tripping you up. The way I see it, if we get rid of this thing, then you have no more excuses. You have to come with me. And who knows? Maybe you'll actually have some fun, too."

"I'm sorry." I mean it. I didn't realize how much she hated staying home because of me. Plus, she's right—I never wanted to go to the pool or mini golfing or skating with her. It's much safer for me to stay at home, cataloguing my Robo-Warrior cards.

Declining all those hangout invitations doesn't hurt Sharkey's social life the same way it does mine, though. Everyone still loves to be around her—star Wyld Beasts crew member—at school. Unfortunately for me, being the star faceplanter doesn't hold the same draw.

Sharkey sighs. "It's okay. But we're going to get rid of this bad luck business, and you're going to do all the stuff I want to do. You owe me. Deal?"

I shrug. "Deal."

Sharkey's mouth curves into a satisfied smirk, but it falters a little when I push the clunky phone toward her.

"Your good feeling, your luck, you dial," I say.

She picks up the receiver. She puts it on speaker mode, and I read the Nevada phone number aloud as she pokes at the keypad.

The phone rings. I bite my lip. Sharkey blows out an

upward breath, sending her bangs fluttering. Ramon folds his arms, his expression unreadable.

"Oasis Elder Care!" a woman chirps on the other line.

Elder care? That's a promising start. Ramon's friend would sure be elder.

I lean toward the cell phone and project my voice. "I'm trying to reach Domingo Agustin."

"One moment, please!"

Smooth jazz sails through the receiver while we're on hold. It's cut off abruptly by a "hello?" A man, but with a voice too young and clear to be as old as Ramon and Apong Rosing.

I clear my throat. "Hi, we're looking for Domingo Agustin."

"Are you a telemarketer?"

Sharkey rolls her eyes. "No, we're in seventh grade. We're doing a school project on Filipino World War II veterans and how they've had to fight for the benefits the US government promised. We're hoping to interview a Domingo Agustin."

Even with her ankle sprain drawing half her attention, Sharkey's words come out so naturally I almost believe them. I envy her ability to fudge the truth like that. Lying requires a somewhat believable story and a whole lot of luck, and luck is something I obviously can never count on.

The voice on the other side of the line pauses. "Hold on, I'm going to put you on speaker."

Some muffled motions come through the line. I catch the tail end of the man who answered the phone explaining the school project to someone else.

A new voice, an older man, speaks up. "Hello?"

I lean closer to the phone. "Hi, is this Domingo Agustin, from the Philippines? From Santa Maria?"

"Yes, yes, it is," the man replies.

My hope surges when I hear that same hint of an accent that Ramon and Apong Rosing have.

Ramon goes still.

"And did you serve in World War II?" I not only want to make sure it's the right Ingo, but to also keep up the cover story of the school project. There's a lot of background noise coming through the speaker, and I get the sense that whoever answered the phone isn't too far away. Starting off with "if you're the right guy, I need you to break this curse!" is a surefire way to a quick hang-up and block-caller.

"Yes, I did serve in the war."

My hands go clammy. I know I shouldn't dare hope that this is the Ingo we've been searching for. But with Sharkey hovering over the phone and Ramon's wide grin, it's tough to keep the excitement down. "And did you know a Ramon Ruiz?"

The pause that follows dulls the hopeful glint in Ramon's eyes.

"It's Ingo, I know it," Ramon whispers. But even though his words are confident, the pinch of his brow speaks otherwise.

"What did you say?" the older man asks after a moment.

I'm almost certain that the man knows exactly what I said, but I repeat myself anyway.

"Who told you to call here?" the man yells suddenly, his voice frantic. "Who are you? Tell me!"

There's some distant mumbling on the other side of the line, and it doesn't sound happy. The sound on the call suddenly gets clearer, as if we've been taken off speakerphone.

"You've upset my father," the younger man who answered the phone says. "You'd better not be those scammers pretending to be from the bank. I filed a police report the first time, so if you think—"

"Us? Scammers?" Sharkey interrupts, her face twisted in confusion.

My brain scrambles to come up with a response. "We're not trying to scam anyone! We really need to talk to Ingo to—"

"Stop right there," the man barks. Then he sighs heavily, and his voice comes out calmer, but firm. "Look, kids. It isn't a good day for this. I'm sorry, but my father's not going to be able to help you on your project. You'll have to find someone else."

"But—" Sharkey, Ramon, and I begin at the same time.

"No. And don't call here again."

SEVENTEEN

"**T**HAT WAS INGO," RAMON SAYS. "I AM SURE OF THIS."
I uncross my legs and push myself up to standing.
"Then why was he so upset when we mentioned you?"

If somehow Sharkey and I lost touch and someone called me up seventy years later about it, I'd want to catch up. How can this be the same Ingo that was Ramon's best friend?

Ramon crosses his arms. "I'm a ghost, not a mind reader. If you hadn't scared him away, we could have—"

"I didn't scare him away," I say. "It's not my fault the mention of your name upset someone who's supposed to be your best friend."

Ramon's eyes narrow into a fiery glare, but I don't back down. Finding Ingo is just as important to me—maybe even more so. It's not like Ramon's going to die *again*.

Besides, this Ruiz family curse goes all the way back to

Ramon's time. Ramon had the same thirteen days to fix it. I know he's probably hurt at that man's reaction, but he has no right to be angry at me.

"Can we focus, please?" Sharkey cuts in. With her sprain keeping her stuck at the desk, her patience must be paper thin. "If you're absolutely sure that this Domingo Agustin is the right Ingo, then we should look up his address at this Oasis place."

I blow out a breath, letting some of my bad mood go with it. I grab Dad's laptop off my nightstand. Normally, my parents wouldn't let me use this without a good school-assignment-based reason. But apparently they trust super-responsible Sharkey enough to keep an eye on me this afternoon. (I'm a little bit insulted by that.)

I brush a few crumbs off it and pull up the internet browser. No replies to any of my dozen emails to Uncle Ritchie yet. I'd be more disappointed if we didn't have this solid lead.

It takes less than a minute to find the address of Oasis Elder Care in Henderson, Nevada.

I angle the laptop to show Sharkey and Ramon. In his excitement, Ramon tries to grab it.

"Perfect," Sharkey says. "You can just mail Ramon and the amulet to this Oasis place, right, Freddie? Curse broken, problem solved."

Both Ramon and I frown at the idea.

"I don't know about mailing it," I say.

Ramon nods. "It's too risky. With our luck, I could get lost for another ten years."

"And I won't have another ten years if I don't stop this curse countdown." I start to pace, my fingers running along the five notches on the amulet. That means eight more days of spirits trying to ruin everything, then kill me.

Even safely hunkered down at home today, I've managed to rip my pajama pants right down the backside, spill mouthwash all over the bathroom rug, and shatter a shelf in our refrigerator. I had to move all the food out so I could clean up the glass. I nicked myself twice, and I've got the Robo-Warrior Band-Aids to prove it. "Where is Henderson, anyway?"

Sharkey tugs the laptop closer to her and pulls up a map. "It's a city right next to Las Vegas! Sixteen miles away."

I raise my eyebrow at the weird excitement in her voice.

"My Spring Showcase is in Las Vegas! Looks like these ancient spirits don't know enough about American geography to stop us. I can just bring the amulet with . . ." Her voice fades as she glances down at her wrapped ankle. "Oh. Those spirits sure are thorough."

I plop down onto my bed facedown, angling just enough

to groan out of the corner of my mouth. "I don't know how I'm going to get to Henderson in eight days."

"Family vacation to Las Vegas?" Sharkey suggests.

"Then I can navigate to this Oasis place from there," Ramon offers. "I have an excellent sense of direction."

I can almost hear Dad's "no, we don't have the money for that" ringing in my ears. He already grumbled about buying me a whole new set of school uniforms after my pen explosion. My parents for sure won't be up for a spontaneous trip to another state, especially for reasons I don't want to tell them about.

"Take the bus?"

"Even if I had the cash for a bus ticket, my parents would literally kill me for disappearing to Henderson on my own." I push up onto my elbows. "You sure you're not an evil spirit, Sharkey? Because your suggestion's a guaranteed way to end my existence before my thirteen days are up."

I'm joking, but the thought of the curse dealing me a fatal blow sends cracks through my determination. It's not nearly as shattering as the shriek that tears from the kitchen.

"Freddie!" Mom yells, in that increasingly loud you're-in-big-trouble tone. "Why are all our groceries on the kitchen floor?"

———————

A knock on the door interrupts my math worksheet. Homework on a Saturday night is Mom's punishment for me ruining a week's worth of groceries after the refrigerator shelf broke. I didn't even have homework from school. Mom purposely printed extra worksheets from some torture website just for this.

And Ramon, the math whiz that he is, isn't around to help me out. He's been with Apong Rosing since this afternoon, gossiping about some town mate neither of them have seen in ages.

I set down my pencil. My wooden chair squeaks as I lean back. "Come in."

Mom peeks in. "Your Auntie Sisi and Sharlene brought over dinner. Come eat while it's hot."

I smile at the thought that I'm off the hook, but then Mom adds, "You can finish your math later."

Still, I welcome the distraction and the scent of fried chicken that's slowly filling the house.

Sharkey's already on the couch, holding a paper plate piled high with store-bought chicken and coleslaw and home-cooked white rice. Her mouth is full, so she throws me an upward head nod, then turns her attention back to the television. One of the Lord of the Rings movies is on.

Being kicked out to the living room with dinner means that Auntie Sisi, Mom, and Apong Rosing are doing their adults-talking-and-ignoring-us thing. Fine with me. Maybe Mom will forget about the math worksheets. Or maybe Ramon will get so bored tagging along with Apong that he'll finish my worksheets for fun.

I load up my plate, tuck the banana ketchup bottle under my arm, and join Sharkey in front of the television. I sink into the green armchair and set to work extracting a shiny red gob of banana ketchup from the bottle.

On the television, the characters pledge to help Frodo journey to destroy the ring. What I wouldn't do for a group of magical creatures to ferry me to Las Vegas right now. I could do without being chased by orcs and Ringwraiths, though.

Out of the corner of my eye, I see Sharkey staring at me. She has a huge grin.

Suspicious, I pause before taking a bite of the chicken. "What, did you do something to this?"

Sharkey peers at the adults in the kitchen, then whispers, "I have the best idea. The Spring Showcase next weekend."

Glad that at least there isn't anything wrong with my chicken, I tear off a piece of drumstick and dunk it in the ketchup. "We went through this. Your ankle. You can't dance."

She blows a breath upward, sending her bangs flitting around. "I know, I know. The swelling has gone down, but

Auntie Alice said no running or jumping or dancing for a while." Sharkey has the energy of a nuclear bomb. Ordering her not to run, jump, dance, or even walk at a brisk pace is a nightmare for her.

"Sorry. I know you were really excited about it." I gesture to the television with the drumstick in my hand. "Plus it would've really helped me out if you could've hobbited the amulet over to Ingo like these guys."

"That's my amazing idea! We can still get to Mordor!"

I pause midbite. "But Auntie Alice said you can't compete," I say around a cheekful of rice.

She leans forward, her eyes and grin wide and eerily Gollum-like. I should've known I wasn't going to like what she was going to say next. "I can't. But you can. You can be my sub on the Wyld Beasts! Spring Showcase will get us close to Las Vegas, and then we'll just have to find a way to skip over to Henderson."

I nearly choke on chicken and laughter. Wyld Beasts didn't want me when I auditioned, but she wants me to dance with them in front of all the top dancers on this side of the country at the Spring Showcase? I rub my hip like it still hurts from that audition tumble.

"No way. You all won awards this year. I can't even make it through five choreographed steps in an elf costume for a Christmas pageant." I shake my head and gulp down the overchewed chicken. "And doesn't the Wyld Beasts have subs?"

"We're short on kids. The Evans twins can't come because of some big family reunion."

The chicken plunks into my stomach like a rock. Or maybe it's the dread of even considering Sharkey's plan. "Your teammates aren't going to want me anywhere near them."

"Let me worry about them. You focus on remembering the piece. You didn't do too badly at the audition, besides accidentally clobbering the other kids. But if I'm going to vouch for you, you've got to be perfect. And not so . . . hazardous."

The slight insult would probably have hurt more if it wasn't true. "And what about the curse? There's no way I'll get through the audition without tripping over myself or clotheslining some other kid."

I don't need to give everyone more of a reason to avoid me. Ruining Spring Showcase for some of the coolest kids at Holy Redeemer? I'd never live this down.

Her face twists in annoyance. "Freddie, I'm going out on a limb here to save you. You're really going to say no before you even try?"

"I have tried before!" I growl. She doesn't know what

it's like to always count yourself out of something because a curse will find a way to mess you up. "It gets exhausting to always be *trying*. Sometimes I just want to *do*, like everyone else."

"Come on, Freddie." She sounds softer this time. "It's time to be brave. You can't let this curse run your life."

I drop my bare drumstick bone onto my plate. Turning off that part of my brain—the part that says I can't, I shouldn't, I won't—isn't as easy as Sharkey thinks it is. For me, trying means I end up failing. Trying with the best intentions and four-leaf clovers and rabbit's-foot keychains in my pocket? Also failing. She's hopeful that things will be different this time, but I'm not so sure.

But she's right: I can't let the curse run the show, especially if it will get worse and worse and kill me. This dance crew plan is going to be a disaster, both socially and to my poor uncoordinated appendages, but I can't afford to turn it down. My somersaulting stomach makes the decision for me.

Sharkey's honed her ability to detect my defeat based on even tiny body language changes. My chin dips in the slightest of nods, and she practically beams.

I cut her off before she can claim victory. "Even if, by some miracle, I make the team, that doesn't solve our biggest problem. How are we supposed to pay for all this? The hotels alone are going to be—" I actually have no idea how much hotels in Las Vegas cost. "Really expensive."

Sharkey's victory smile starts to creep onto her face, and she shoves me hard on the arm like we're in on some joke together (we're not). "Wyld Beasts collects fees for this kind of stuff every month, and I'm all paid up. But here's the best part: Dale's dad's company is the team sponsor for the show-case! That's why our costumes have those big Eastside Pizza logos on the back. Our hotel rooms are paid for!"

My resistance starts to crumble like the dry crusts of those awful Eastside Pizza pizzas. "If you think this will work . . ."

"It will. I'll be your teacher."

I can almost see Sharkey now, clapping to the made-up beat in her head, giddy on power.

"But you have to really try, okay?" she adds carefully. "This is my dance crew. You can't embarrass me."

I scowl, even though I understand where she's coming from. "My life depends on it, in case you forgot."

The triumph in her voice is as subtle as an air horn. "Good. I'm going to send you our choreography video so you can drill it into your head, and I'll start preparing for our first lesson. Tomorrow. Not a second to waste, right?"

As the TV commercial ends and Frodo's terrified face

splays across the screen, it occurs to me that this whole thing —Ingo being in Nevada, the dance competition being there next weekend—might not be the nice twist of fortune it appears to be.

Maybe it's all part of the bad luck.

EIGHTEEN

*H*EAT RIPPLES OFF THE CONCRETE OF OUR DRIVEWAY.
The white-toothed morning newscaster warned that it'd be unseasonably warm today. And of course it's the day that Sharkey and I start our dance practice.

I grimace at the bead of sweat rolling down my neck. But either we practice here, in the hot but secluded space between our houses, or in the cooler rooms indoors, in front of my parents. I take a sip from my apple juice box and instantly regret it. The juice is the temperature of a bath.

In the thinning shadow of the garage, Sharkey leans against the wall, one arm slung over a crutch, the other cradling her cell phone. Already bobbing her head, she taps at her screen and music blares out.

I shake the nervous energy out of my arms. I smooth

down one of the Robo-Warrior Band-Aids coming loose around my finger and bounce my barely used cross-trainers against the concrete. "Was this song always this fast?"

Sharkey rolls her eyes. "It's the same song you auditioned to. You did watch the choreography video, right?"

"A dozen times."

According to Sharkey, the Wyld Beasts' choreographer built part of their Spring Showcase performance off the audition song. He added a lot more complex and adventurous moves, none of which I'm going to even attempt right now. Then he posted the video on the group's private page, for those who couldn't make it to practice. Absences are no excuse for mistakes in the Wyld Beasts crew.

"Only a dozen?" Her eyebrows scrunch together in concern. "Well, let's just try to get through the basics of that first minute. For now, you only need to be good enough to fool the team into letting you take my place."

Ramon, projecting himself next to Sharkey, chuckles. "I'd say good luck, but—"

"As long as you don't say 'break a leg,'" Sharkey cuts in. "With your curse, it might just happen."

My shoulders tense at the reminder of just how dangerous being a Ruiz can be. I feel awful enough about Sharkey's twisted ankle.

I owe it to her to dance my heart out, if it gets me to Oasis, Ingo, and the end of this curse. But that doesn't change the fact that my stomach is doing backflips.

"What if I can't do this?" I ask. "What if I'm not good enough to get on the team? I wasn't the first time."

Sharkey sighs, and her bangs do their fluttery dance. "I wouldn't risk you messing up Spring Showcase for my team if I didn't think you could do this."

"Just try, Freddie," Ramon urges. "I sense no spirits around right now, if that helps."

It does make me feel better, knowing there isn't some mean spirit waiting to literally or figuratively trip me up. I nod, and Sharkey restarts the song. I try out the first few moves of the piece. Thankfully, Sharkey has spared me from having to learn the more daring moves she's usually responsible for: I'd break my neck trying to execute a handspring for sure.

But even getting to the places I'm supposed to be at each beat of the song is proving tricky. I nearly stumble over my own feet a few times. I consider it a miracle that I don't end up with two sprained ankles after the first run-through.

Both Sharkey and Ramon look like they've bitten into chocolate chip cookies only to find that they were oatmeal raisin instead.

"Well?" I pump in a few rapid-fire breaths.

"That was . . ." Ramon waves his hand in the air like he's trying to stir up the right word. "Indeed dancing, of some sort."

I wipe the sweat from my brow. "Of some sort?"

Sharkey groans and slaps a hand to her forehead. "What have I done?"

My shoulders sag. "I wasn't that bad, was I?"

"My team is going to hate me!" She shakes her head, her palm still covering her face. "Stick a fork in my social life. It's done."

I drag a hand through my hair, flicking off a couple more beads of sweat. "You two are the ones who said I should try!" I know it's only my first day practicing this piece I'd learned months ago, but I don't have the time to perfect it. The competition is next weekend. I'm trying out tomorrow afternoon so I can join the group for their last week of rehearsals.

I snap up my warm juice box again and drain the last of it. Channeling all my frustration into my fingers, I crush the empty box and chuck it at the garbage can nearby. I miss. I swear that a crow perched on top of the garage laughs at me.

"You cannot be so discouraged. You're simply warming up," Ramon says gently. "You did this before, correct? And you must have done well enough to not maim yourself then."

Another one of Ramon's weirdly phrased compliments, but I'll take it.

Sharkey finally lowers her hand from her face. "Okay, we can salvage this. You audition tomorrow. So we'll practice tonight after dinner and tomorrow morning before school. And promise you'll watch that video at least a dozen more times before bed."

I lean back against the garage and let my head thunk against the wall. "We can practice day and night, but let's face it: with my luck, I'm not getting on that crew."

Sharkey shakes her head, like she's trying to keep my words from worming into her ears. "Luck's only part of it. The rest of it is going to be good old-fashioned wheeling and dealing. Dale knows he's in a bind with me and the Evans twins out. As long as you get through the piece without falling or tripping one of the other kids, we'll find a way to stow you in the back somewhere."

I twist to look at her straight-on. "Without falling or tripping? This is me we're talking about. I've got an expiration date a week away. How can I possibly expect to ace this audition and dodge these spirits that are after us?"

"Snap out of it, Freddie." Ramon plants his hands on his hips and glares at me like a drill sergeant. "Sometimes it's not about luck. Sometimes it's about skill, about smarts. You can't use the curse as an excuse for all the bad things that happen to you. You can't use it as an excuse not to try."

"But my whole life, I've—"

"And that's precisely it." Ramon wags a translucent finger at me. "It isn't always about good luck or bad luck. Sometimes it's just life. And good things and bad things are going to happen, no matter what we do. If I hadn't—" His eyes go a little glassy, and his voice softens then. "If I hadn't died, I wouldn't have stopped trying to get the anting-anting back in Ingo's hands. I wouldn't have given up."

Even if I had something to snap back at him with, I wouldn't have. He looks too sad, with his downturned lips and distant eyes.

And Ramon has a point. As frustrated as I am, I can't afford to give up. Not only has the curse managed to wreck countless days over the past twelve years, but who knows how bad it's going to get in the next few days? I can't risk myself or anyone else getting hurt. Or worse.

I have the power to fix this. Ramon doesn't. With our combined skills and smarts, as Ramon put it, we might stand a chance against these spirits. All I have to do is get good enough to fade into the background of a break-dancing performance.

The first step is trying.

And even if I make a fool of myself or somehow knock myself unconscious with a dance move, which—let's be real —is very likely, then the second step is trying again. My life is at stake here.

I push off against the wall. I take my spot on the asphalt a few feet away.

"Let's try again," I say, motioning to Sharkey's silent phone. "Play the song."

NINETEEN

I HATE WHEN PEOPLE STARE AT ME. UNFORTUNATELY, I FIND myself in a lot of situations in which all eyes end up on me. Like when I toppled a baby food display at the grocery store, sending pureed green peas and tiny glass shards everywhere. Or when the paint bottle in art class decided to unclog over my face, leaving a Freddie-shaped outline on the bulletin board behind me. Or now, as I'm clutching Sharkey's backpack while she leads me into the band room after school.

My stomach churns as I walk into the den of the Wyld Beasts dance crew. The crew members lounge lazily on red plastic chairs that have been pushed to the edge of the room. A couple kids toy with the audio system, a massive, decade-old speaker wired up to a tabletop of buttons and blinking lights. Bone-thumping music cuts in and out as they try to sync their cell phones to the system. All of that stops when Sharkey and I enter. I'm a magnet for the eyes of the nine other kids in the room.

Dale stalks across the floor, his gold curls bouncing like he's in a shampoo commercial. Now that school's over, we've all changed out of our uniforms for practice. Dale's exchanged his blue slacks and white collared shirt for green pants with a white stripe down the side and a bright red shirt with a blocky Robo-Warrior printed on it.

I know exactly which Robo-Warrior that is: Brackiac, the poison-wielding swamp dweller. Stellar attack stats, but poor defense abilities. I'm about to comment on it when the distaste on Dale's face makes me think twice about being friendly.

The edges of Dale's lips dip down as he takes in Sharkey's crutch and wrapped ankle. "So your aunt is positive you can't dance with us this weekend?"

Sharkey shrugs coolly. "I'm out of commission. But lucky for you, I've found a replacement." She sweeps out an arm like a magician doing her big reveal.

But she's not pulling a rabbit out of a hat. She's pointing at me—bad-luck-from-head-to-toe me.

I swallow the huge lump of worry, sending it plummeting into my overactive stomach, and wave at the group. I am a hundred percent sure that the move came off awkwardly. I then attempt a casual "hey," only to have my voice break and the tone change midword.

I wish I could sink straight through the floor.

Dale's gaze sweeps over me, then pins on Sharkey. "Is this a joke? It's the Spring Showcase, and you want to sub in Faceplant Freddie?"

I wince. I need to smooth over that second-grade mishap, and all the ones after that, to even get a chance to audition for the team. "Your piece calls for ten dancers, Dale," I say. "You're short one."

"It'll mess up the whole look of the piece. No symmetry, no balance," Sharkey adds.

A couple of the other Wyld Beasts bob their heads in agreement, as if symmetry and balance are in some martial arts code they live by.

Sharkey sticks a thumb out in my direction. "I'm supposed to stay off my feet, so unless you want me sitting in a chair behind everyone, you'll be better off with him."

I inch forward. "She taught me all the changes from the audition piece. I've been practicing nonstop." I leave out the fact that those practices only started a day or so ago and that they mostly involved me dancing terribly.

Whispers float through the room. Some of the crew seem curious.

Sharkey huffs. "Dale, just let him audition. You got somewhere better to be right now?"

Dale steps back. "Fine. Show us what you've got, Faceplant Freddie."

With a nod from Sharkey, I shuffle to the middle of the room. I try to kill the butterflies tornadoing in my stomach while Sharkey pulls out her phone and connects it to the audio system. Even after all those hours of practice, I'm not sure I can do this. But it's too late to back out now.

"I do not sense any spirits around," Ramon says from the amulet at my neck. "Don't worry about the curse right now. You can do this."

That's easy to say when you're nice and cozy in that coin, I want to answer back.

I need to concentrate. I have to prove to the Wyld Beasts that I can do this so I can get to Las Vegas and closer to Ingo. Ignoring the storm clouds roiling in my gut, I train every brain cell on moving my limbs without falling over or smacking someone in the face by accident.

The music starts, and I let the muscle memory take over. Just like I practiced dozens of times. Nothing fancy, no extra flourishes. I stick to the choreography, like it's a sequence in a video game and Dale is the big boss to beat.

The footwork comes to me almost mechanically, thanks to all the work Sharkey and I put in. Despite her urging me to test my limits, I drew the line at those handsprings and flips —I don't trust my luck to hold that much. With each practiced move, my ash heap of confidence rekindles. Not a bonfire, but at least a spark. I start to believe that I might actually pull this off after all. With skills and smarts, like Ramon said.

The beat bumps in my bones. As the song goes on, a couple of the other kids bob their heads, their faces more open and amused than judging. It's a good sign that I'm winning them over with my somewhat competent performance.

I've spent all this time avoiding activities like this because of the curse. I never wanted to risk the injury or the sheer embarrassment—middle schoolers never forget. But with Ramon's reassurance that the spirits are nowhere to be seen, I can let loose a little.

By the end, I'm almost smiling. I'm almost having fun.

And that's when it happens. The rumble in my stomach that I thought had been nerves? It occurs to me that it might've actually been the deep-fried bean burrito I ate for lunch.

The final big-finish pose is a deep squat, leaned back, with my arms crossed. I execute it exactly as planned.

What *isn't* planned is the music-stopping, social-life-killing fart I let loose. The sound reverberates through the room, like the elephants trumpeting at the zoo, stopping all the other wildlife in their tracks.

The Wyld Beasts transform into a pack of cackling hye-nas as I leap up. Sharkey, a shade of mortified pink I haven't seen before, looks torn between congratulating me and pre-tending I followed her in off the street. Ramon laughs so hard he's wheezing, and I'm thankful that, other than Shar-key, no one else in this room can hear him. Dale's pinched face tells me he's not as amused as the rest of the crew.

This is exactly what I feared would go wrong—a room-ful of people making fun of me. I can't believe I let Sharkey and Ramon talk me into this. It'll be a miracle if anyone at school comes within ten feet of me after today.

I'm about to dash for the nearest exit when Dale stalks over. "You think this is a joke, Freddie? Our crew's got a reputation to uphold. You might be used to being a laugh-ingstock, but I—"

Before I can open my mouth to defend myself, Layla, swimming in her oversize gray sweater, speaks up. "Cut 'im some slack, Dale. Freddie did fine. He's as good a replace-ment as we're going to get right now. And I doubt he's going to, um, improvise like that at the showcase."

A few of the other kids who aren't still doubled over laughing murmur in agreement. I wasn't expecting this sup-port. "As good as we're going to get right now" is as much as I could have hoped for. It takes some of the sting out of what I'd thought was the worst audition of all time, even worse than the one where I took down a third of the team. I hide the nervousness of my gaze by swiping my forearm across my sweat-slicked brow.

Dale stares down at me like I'm gum stuck to the bottom of his shoe. "I'd rather risk that symmetry and balance stuff than let you mess it all up for us."

"I won't mess up. You saw for yourself I could do it."

Dale snorts. "So? Maybe you got lucky."

He doesn't know how wrong he is, but I don't have the time or patience to correct him.

"What if you trip up at the showcase?" he adds. "You're not exactly known for your reflexes. Didn't you get smacked in the head with a soccer ball?"

The blood rushes to my face. How is everyone keeping such great track of my injuries? Half these kids forgot their permission slips for our aquarium field trip.

I'm losing ground here. I need to get to Las Vegas, and Dale is the only thing standing in my way right now.

"How about I give you my allowance for a month?" I offer.

"But you don't get an . . . Oh," Sharkey says, zipping her lips too late.

Dale glares at me.

I shove my hands in my pockets. "Your social studies homework? I can help you with it."

Dale snorts. "Nice try. I've already got a solid A in social studies. I don't even need extra credit."

He smirks like he's holding candy over a toddler's head, and my traitorous stomach churns again. I need to find a way to convince Dale to let me on the team.

"Well?" Dale crosses his arms. His forearms rest right on top of the Robo-Warrior Brackiac decal on his shirt.

That gives me an idea, one I don't like a single bit. But my chances for getting on the team and hitching a ride to the showcase are shrinking by the second.

"How about we play for it?" I grab my backpack and pull out my Robo-Warrior deck. I slip the cards out of their protective case. "I win, I'm on the crew."

Dale rolls his eyes. "Oh please. I've seen you play at the Tuesday group by the gym."

He won't go as far as admitting he knows I'd win—I really am that good—and I can tell he's not going to let himself get beaten in front of his friends.

"Then how about I give you a rare card, and you let me onto the crew?"

Dale scowls and plants an indignant hand on his hips. "Come on, Freddie. You think you can just bribe your way onto the Wyld Beasts? What kind of—"

"Okay, okay." I put my hands out to calm him. The gears in my brain whir. I see him hungrily eyeing my Robo-Warrior deck like it's a slice of Eastside Pizza, but he's not going to take a direct exchange for a spot for me to go to Las Vegas. The thought of Las Vegas kicks those brain gears into thinking about odds. There might be another way to play off Dale's Robo-Warrior fandom.

I flip over the deck and fan it out, logo side up so no one can tell which card is which. "Then how about this: I let you take three cards. If any of them are rare cards, then I'm on the team. It's all chance. No bribing, no—what's it called —squid pro quo."

Sharkey shuffles next to me. "What are you doing?" she asks.

She knows how precious this deck is to me. I've spent years building it up, which was especially difficult with my bad luck doling me packs of mostly boring cards. In my hands is many Christmases' and birthdays' worth of gifts, as well as countless hours of way-below-minimum-wage yard work at Sharkey's house. Almost every cent I get goes into collecting Robo-Warrior packs. And every now and then, when the sun is shining and the curse hiccups, I get a rare ultrapowerful card.

It's my usual awful luck I'm banking on now. There's no way Dale will be able to pick three dud cards. We'll make this deal, he'll get a card he loves, and I get on the team. If I lose this shot at a Las Vegas trip, complete with sponsorship and Spring Showcase cover story, I don't know if I'll ever make it out to see Ingo before the spirits get me.

"I got this," I whisper to her before turning back to Dale. "Come on. Three cards. If none of them are rare, then I'm not on the team and I never audition again. It's that simple. What've you got to lose?"

I flash the deck at him and tilt my chin with enough challenge to draw Dale's attention. Dale huffs as if this idea is ridiculous, but the greedy glint in his eye tells me I've reeled him in.

"You probably don't even have any rare cards in that huge deck," he mutters, but his eyes stay on the fanned-out cards. "But hey, if this means I get three free cards and you not on the team, then I'm game."

He rubs his palms together, then inspects the uniform gold and black tops of the deck. He plucks the first card.

I hold my breath.

He smiles wide.

The Ruiz family curse does not disappoint.

"A knockout card," Layla says reverently. "I've only ever seen that played once before, in a tournament at the mall."

I bite back a groan. That was the first rare card I ever collected. I went through two dozen packs of normal cards before I pulled out this foil-embossed one.

A smugness sweeps across Dale's face. "Nice. I could use one of these."

"Congratulations, you've got your rare card," I grumble, starting to straighten the deck to put it away. "Now am I on the crew?"

Dale slaps a hand on my wrist. "Nuh-uh. You said three cards, Ruiz. I get two more."

I grit my teeth. I don't know what hurts more: the unforgettable fart I ended my audition on or the thought of losing two more cards. "Am I on the crew?"

Layla pats me on the shoulder. "Of course you are. Right, Dale? A deal's a deal."

Dale puckers like he's bit into a lemon, but he nods. "Yeah, you're on the crew. But I still get those two cards."

Those two cards end up being the most powerful ones left in my deck: a hitpoint booster and a resurrection card. All that time and money poured into a Robo-Warrior card collection, gone in the blink of an eye.

Ramon sighs with relief from the amulet. Getting on the team means we're on our way to Ingo and his curse-breaking power. And once those evil spirits stop looking my way, maybe I can pick up a few more rare cards.

Dale tucks the cards into his backpack and claps his hands together. The rest of the crew rise from their spots around the room and head to the middle of the makeshift dance floor.

I jog over to Sharkey, who's plopped down into one of the empty red chairs by the wall. I doubt Ramon wants to be bonked around his cell any more than he has been during the audition. I lift the amulet up and over my head and hand it to her. Seven notches glint in the harsh band room lighting. Only six more days to break this curse.

"Decent performance, Freddie," Ramon chirps from the amulet. "You do not shame the Ruiz family name."

"Thanks?"

"Don't mess up," Sharkey says, her hand closing tight over the coin. "It's my reputation, my crew on the line here."

And my *life*. "I'll do my best."

She nods as Dale positions me in the back of the formation. She watches me like a hawk all practice, then spends the entire car ride home lecturing me about every too-slow move, every missed beat. And I've got one more week of this fun. Lucky me.

TWENTY

THE FRESH-CUT WOOD SMELL OF THE HOME IMPROVEMENT
Center tickles my nose, and for the tenth time in a minute, I fight back a sneeze.

The Home Improvement Center is a massive warehouse with sky-high shelves packed with everything you need to improve (or ruin) your home. Power tools for every type of job, enough lumber to recreate a forest, a thousand different kinds of screws. Dad said we'd only be here five minutes, but we're rounding on half an hour now. Ever since Dad was laid off and started his own business, we've spent way too much time zigzagging these aisles. I'll consider this trip short if we're out of here before the store closes.

Down the aisle, he's comparing different paintbrushes. I busy myself with paint color sample cards, which are only slightly more interesting than what he's looking at. I don't dare move any closer to the aisles with the lightbulbs and saw blades. I've tested my luck enough this week.

"Go talk to him!" Ramon urges. He's projected himself next to the cardboard cutout of the Home Improvement Hippo mascot. He leans an elbow on the upright, flannel-clad hippopotamus's shoulder, like they're best friends posing for a photo.

"He's busy!" I whisper back harshly.

"You have to tell him soon. How else are we going to get to this Henderson city? Can you drive?"

I roll my eyes at him. "I'm twelve."

"So?"

A green-aproned employee strolling by raises an eyebrow at the sight of me talking to a cardboard hippo. I offer a weak smile, like this is some zany thing kids do all the time, then glare at Ramon when she's gone.

"I'll ask him. Just leave me alone," I mumble.

"Be brave!"

"Be gone."

Ramon disappears back into the amulet.

I don't want to bother Dad while he's still inspecting paintbrushes, so I pick up the Cucumber Green paint sample card to take another look. And, of course, I somehow manage to pull out the entire stack of Cucumber Greens, sending dozens of thin cards scattering onto the concrete floor.

I lunge to gather them up, only to smack my forehead on the bottom of the card display. Then all the sneezes I've been fighting avalanche out so hard, the green-aproned employee comes sprinting back.

She peers down at me, her black curls curtaining around her face. She looks torn between concern and being grossed out by a possibly plague-ridden customer. "Are you okay?"

I wave the sloppy stack of cards in my hand at her. "I'b fide. All udder codtrol."

I smile awkwardly at her again. If she didn't think I was weird already, she does now.

She nods unsurely and returns to the paint department help desk, keeping a worried eye on me the whole time.

Ramon laughs from inside the amulet.

"Not. One. Word," I say through gritted teeth. I shove the Cucumber Greens back into their slot on the color display right as my dad appears beside me.

"Who are you talking to?" he asks.

Caught talking to my trapped great-granduncle twice in the span of ten minutes? I can't even blame the curse for this. It's my own sloppiness.

"Just reading the weird names of the paints. Not One Word Green. Funny, right?" I lie. I angle myself between him and the paint display. "Ready to go?"

Back in the truck, I finally rally enough courage to ask

him about Spring Showcase. We're trapped in here together for the ten-minute ride home. Better to ask him now, before we're around Mom and get her opinion too.

"Great news!" I try my best to sound thrilled, even as the worry sits as heavy as the Home Improvement Hippo in the pit of my stomach. "I got onto the Wyld Beasts dance crew!"

He slaps an encouraging hand on my shoulder without taking his eyes off the road. "That *is* great news. That's your cousin's dance crew, right? I didn't even know you were interested in that stuff. Good for you, finally trying new things and meeting other kids."

I laugh nervously. "Yeah, well, with her twisted ankle, they needed one more person for their crew for the Spring Showcase next Sunday . . ." I pause long enough to brace myself. "In Las Vegas."

"What?" Dad brakes at the stop sign a little too hard and my head whips forward.

I shift in my seat. "The American Youth Break-Dancing Organization's regional showcase. It's where the best dance crews of the Pacific Coast and Southwest perform and compete for the prestigious Peacock Cup." I recite what's on the organization's website word for word. I memorized it earlier (and even thought about writing it on my arm).

Dad sighs. "But today's Monday."

I keep my voice cheerful. "Yup."

"And the showcase is this weekend?"

"Yup."

"In Las Vegas."

"Yup."

"This dance crew—they absolutely need you?"

I'm going to need more than a one-word answer to hurry this along. "If they don't have ten people, they're disqualified."

"And you're just telling me now?"

I gulp. "I just got on the crew."

Then he says the words I've been trying to avoid all afternoon. The ones that always strike fear right through my core. "Let's ask your mom."

"No."

I heave an exaggerated sigh and sag my shoulders dramatically. "But, Mom!"

She drops a handful of chopped onions into the hot wok, and they sizzle. "But what?"

Honestly, I don't have a good answer for that. I can't exactly say, *But, Mom, I need to get close to Las Vegas to return an anting-anting and free us and our trapped great-granduncle from a generations-long curse that you don't believe in.* After my parents' reaction during that mess of a spaghetti night last week, I'm certain she'll confiscate the amulet and ground me. I won't live to see the end of that grounding if this curse gets its way.

"But it's the Spring Showcase!"

"For a sport you joined today." She gives the onions a stir with an oversize wooden spoon. "You didn't even tell us you were trying out for the team."

Apong Rosing, word-search puzzle in hand, tsk-tsks in agreement from the dining table. "Always keeping secrets, these children."

"And you expect us to drop everything and take you all the way to Las Vegas?" Mom shakes her head and practically spikes the minced garlic into the wok.

Another tsk-tsk in agreement.

Dad knew exactly what he was doing when he pushed the decision off onto her. That evil genius.

I rest my elbows on the kitchen counter. One elbow lands in a puddle of stray dishwater. "The crew is counting on me."

"I'm glad you're making friends, but who's even on this crew?" Mom asks. "Did someone bully you into this? Is it about some girl?"

"Ugh, Mom, it's nothing like that! Can't I just want to try something new?"

Mom doesn't skip a beat. "Freddie, you never want to

try anything new. Remember when I tried to sign you up for swim club? And golf lessons? And—"

This is going nowhere. In fact, it's going past nowhere. We're firmly in I-want-to-stop-talking-about-this-altogether territory. But I need Mom's go-ahead to get anywhere near Henderson.

Mom's phone blares with the ringtone she has assigned to her boss: a horror-movie-like woman shrieking. She puts up a finger to shush me, then answers, wedging the phone between her ear and her shoulder as she continues cooking.

I lope over to the table and drop into the chair opposite Apong Rosing. The amulet around my neck bumps the table.

Apong glances up from her puzzle at the noise.

I've kept the amulet hidden while at home, but maybe a different approach will work in convincing Mom. Getting Apong on my side could tip the scales. After Ramon's warning, and with her days filled with teleserye episodes and dialysis treatments, I've tried to minimize Apong's share of curse-breaking work. I know she still wants to help, and I need it now more than ever.

I raise the amulet so it catches the fluorescent kitchen light. "We found Ingo. He's in Henderson, Nevada. It's sixteen miles away from Las Vegas," I whisper.

Her eyes widen. "Is that why you are trying to get there? With this dancing-dancing."

"Yes! So I can finally give the amulet back to him. But you know how Mom feels about all this."

A voice sounds next to me, where Ramon has projected himself at a seat at the table. "Rosita, do you know how to operate an automobile? Maybe we don't need his parents' help after all. We can simply wait until the spirits aren't watching and drive ourselves."

Her nose crinkles. "I can drive, but they don't like me to. You bump one little fire hydrant, and suddenly they think you're not fit to have a license."

I bite my tongue. They had to close off half a block for a week because of the flooding caused by her accident. But I'm not about to mention that now, not when I need Apong on our side.

"Can you help me convince Mom? This is my only shot at breaking the curse." I'm not even being dramatic: counting up all the amulet notches so far, I have less than a week left to get Ingo to lift the curse. The thought makes me squirm in my seat.

Apong and I both look to Ramon. He nods: no threat of the spirits right this second. It's safe for my great-grandmother to work her own kind of magic.

Apong gives me a determined smile. "Leave it to me."

She waits until Mom gets off the phone and lifts her

puzzle and pen again, like she's been focused on them the whole time.

"I would like to go to Las Vegas," Apong announces.

Mom whirls around, wooden spoon in hand, to stare at Apong, then me, then back at Apong. She doesn't know what I said to Apong Rosing, but now, if she says no, she's not only saying no to me, but no to her elder grandmother-in-law too.

"But Apong, it's an almost five-hour drive. And—"

"I want to go to Las Vegas!" Apong slaps her puzzle down on the table. The poor kitchen table takes such a beating from this family's strong emotions. "I'm cooped up in this house all day. I deserve a vacation!"

Mom plants one hand on her hip, the other still holding the wooden spoon in the wok. "Your dialysis. It's—"

"Monday, Wednesday, Friday. So I have the whole weekend to enjoy myself."

Mom's brow furrows. "But the expense. We don't have it in our budget to—"

"Actually," I chime in, "Eastside Pizza's covering the crew's hotel rooms."

Mom's eyes flit toward me, like she's just now realizing she's being cornered.

"And I'll pay for the gas. I have the money." Apong tilts

her chin up, almost daring Mom to argue more. "You're always saying Freddie needs to get out of his room and meet new people, try new things. Then when he does, you say no?"

Mom's jaw drops, but no words float out. She's out of excuses. I purse my lips tight to hold back a smile.

We've got her.

After a second, Mom seems to shake out of her shock. "We'll check our work schedules and see who can drive you, Freddie."

I pluck the pink permission slips out of my pocket and drop them onto the table in triumph. "And sign these when you get a chance. Please."

Mom sighs and turns her attention back to her cooking.

The pancit she makes for dinner is the best I've ever had. Maybe because I still taste this victory.

TWENTY-ONE

*H*ITTING THE PAUSE SYMBOL ON THE TABLET SHARKEY lent me, I dab at the sweat on my forehead and billow my shirt to cool down. I pace around my bedroom to catch my breath in between these four-minute dance bursts.

I've cleared a spot in my room where I can practice the Wyld Beasts piece indoors. I hung up some clothes, shoved others into the hamper. I reshelved a few stray books and stuck a stack of old tests and quizzes in the blue recycling bin outside. My floor is now more or less obstacle-free: ideal for cursed kids trying not to break their legs.

I wonder if this is all Sharkey's master plan of getting me to clean my room.

After an hour and a half of practice, in addition to the hour with Wyld Beasts after school, my legs are jelly. I've chugged about a gallon of water and polished off the last drops of orange juice in the house. I hear the piece's song in my head long after it's stopped playing. No wonder Sharkey's always bobbing around and tapping her fingers and toes. This song is going to stay lodged in my head until the day I die.

Which will hopefully not be in four days.

My empty water bottle sits on my desk, and I grab it on the way to the kitchen.

Laughter drifts from the living room as I pass. Apong Rosing and Ramon are watching television again. They're trying to make the most of this unexpected sibling time together, so I've been planting the amulet on the couch next to Apong when I get home from school. Between them catching up after decades apart and my parents off running errands, I've spent the whole afternoon alone, perfecting this performance. I could use a distraction from these grim thoughts of curses and countdowns.

I fill up my water bottle and chug it down to the soundtrack of Apong Rosing and Ramon's chatter. I don't understand the teleserye's Tagalog. I wander into the living room anyway for some quality family time: a good excuse to stop practicing for a moment. Sharkey can't hassle me for spending time with great-grandfolks, can she?

"How is the dancing?" Ramon asks when I stroll in. He's projected on the couch next to Apong Rosing, as if watching

TV together is something they've done for ages. "Are you less embarrassing to Sharkey now?"

I drop into the green armchair. "It's going okay, I guess. I've got the basics down, so hopefully it's enough for them not to kick me off the team before we even get to Vegas."

"Perhaps you can show me your progress, and I can help," Apong suggests.

Ramon shakes his head. "You've already done enough by convincing his parents to take him to the showcase, Rosita. You know you must not become too involved, to keep the spirits from harming you."

The two glare at each other, nonverbally rehashing the same argument I've heard ten times in a matter of days, before Apong Rosing gives a dismissive hmph. "You will do well, Freddie. Music and dance? Those talents run in our family."

So do curses, unfortunately. Her phantom brother splayed out on the couch next to her, oohing and aahing at a luxury cruise line commercial, is proof of that.

"You're not the one being targeted by a bunch of killer spirits, though."

Another dismissive hmph. "I am simply saying you don't need to discourage yourself so much. You may be a Ruiz, but you are also a Ruiz."

I blink, slowly processing what she just said. Yes, I may

have inherited a lifelong streak of bad luck, but so did Dad, Uncle Ritchie, Grandpa Carlo, and Apong Rosing. Dad's construction business is picking up. Despite his business partners' annoyance, Uncle Ritchie's not doing too bad either, connecting American distributors to Filipino manufacturers. Then there's Grandpa Carlo, traveling across the US in a big RV with his third wife. And Apong Rosing raised him all by herself, imparting to him and all of us the Ruiz name, not that of her scoundrel of a common-law husband.

"Yes, Ruizes are cursed," Ramon says, "but we can be bold. You stood up for yourself and for Rosita during that spaghetti dinner, Freddie. It may not involve weapons or hand-to-hand combat"—he balls his hands into fists, like he's ready to box—"but that kind of fight shows bravery. You perhaps need more of it, but you have it in you. Somewhere."

I scan his ghost face for sarcasm but don't find any. "Thanks."

Apong lays a hand on the arm of my chair. "We Ruizes have always had this boldness. You wouldn't be sitting there, sweating all over the furniture, if we all didn't find our own ways to fight the curse."

"Yes, and with this boldness, I believe we can make our own luck," Ramon adds.

Weird pronouncement coming from the ghost, but he

makes a good point. He was bold in enlisting to fight in the war, even if he would've been safer in the mountains with his family. His luck only changed for the worse because he made a mistake.

I frown. "But the curse—"

Apong Rosing snorts. "The curse is a speed bump, not a wall, Freddie. You must find a way to go over it, like we all have. Keep your foot on the gas pedal."

I don't know if Apong should be making driving analogies after that fire-hydrant collision, but I get her point. The curse may have slowed down the Ruizes, but it didn't stop them. Even Ramon is still here, helping me.

A warm feeling spreads in my chest. Is this pride? Pride in the fact that I'm a Ruiz? I've always disliked the fact that I'm part of this cursed family. But looking at Apong Rosing and Ramon now, I realize it's not that bad.

From them, I got my straight black hair and chicken-skin arm bumps. I got my short legs and long torso. And yes, I inherited a family curse, but I also inherited boldness. I inherited bravery. It's in the blood pumping through my veins, the muscles aching from all the dance practice, the sweat that Apong pointed out is ruining our living room armchair. That warm feeling spreads all the way down to my Ruiz toes.

"Thanks," I say. And I mean it. I can make my own luck

too, or I can at least be bold and brave enough to try. All the Ruizes have hit speed bumps over the years. In my hands, this amulet can be the jackhammer we need. It's time for me to tear up the huge speed bump in my own life and clear the path for all Ruizes. Getting good enough at this choreography to keep my spot on the Wyld Beasts is a step in the right direction.

I hop up from the chair, accidentally sloshing around some of the water from my open bottle. "I'm going to get in one more practice before dinner."

I'm a minute into the performance when an eerie shadow darkens my window for a moment. My pulse quickens. I freeze. I can't slip and hurt myself if I'm not even moving, right?

Then there's a crash in the living room.

At first I assume it's yet another twist in Apong Rosing's teleserye—one more person with perfectly timed amnesia? An evil triplet, perhaps?

But Ramon's frantic "Freddie, quick!" has me swinging open my bedroom door.

Apong Rosing's on the rug, her face pinched in pain. She has one elbow propping her up and the other hand on her hip. Ramon is desperately trying to grab her hand to help her, but his limbs go right through hers.

She winces as she tries to rise, so I throw my hands out to stop her. "Stay still! I'll help you."

I dart down the hall toward her. My foot catches on the hallway runner rug and despite the wild windmill of my arms, I stumble and smack shoulder-first into the doorway. The impact sends pain jolting down my bones. I force myself forward, stabilizing my throbbing shoulder with my other hand. It's probably a fraction of what my great-grandmother is feeling, and she's not the one who stoked the wrath of the curse's spirits.

First Sharkey's ankle and now Apong Rosing? Anger burns in the pit of my stomach. These spirits mean business.

But unfortunately for them, so do I. And I've got four days to show them they messed with the wrong family.

TWENTY-TWO

THURSDAY AND FRIDAY BLUR BY IN A HAZE OF SCHOOL, Apong Rosing's doctor appointments, my endless practicing—complete with Sharkey's and Ramon's endless criticism—and two accidental steps into two different piles of dog poop. I'm a bundle of nerves as I walk out the front door Saturday morning, fully dressed in my basketball shorts and marinara-sauce-red Eastside Pizza track jacket.

I'm either going to walk back through this door victorious and free on Sunday night or never walk back through it again.

My mouth goes dry.

I'm not prepared to die. But if we don't get to Ingo, if he doesn't lift this curse? Whether I'm prepared or not, the worst is going to happen.

Mom stands in the driveway next to Uncle Sammy's gray

minivan. She's wearing her faded blue college hoodie and the yoga pants she's had since I was in kindergarten.

Dad is helping Apong Rosing with her seatbelt. Her fall sprained her hip, but she refused to stay home. She bullied her doctor into clearing her to come. Dad and Mom unsuccessfully tried to use her injury as an excuse to cancel the whole Las Vegas trip, which would have canceled my whole life.

Already in the driver's seat, Uncle Sammy is trying to clean off his expensive aviator sunglasses but is only smearing the grime around.

Mom squints against the late-morning sun as I approach. "You have your toothbrush?"

I plunk my duffle bag into the back of the van. "Yes, Mom."

"And extra underwear?"

Who knew a brown kid could turn this pink from embarrassment? A giggle floats out from the other side of the minivan, where Sharkey's saying goodbye to Auntie Sisi and Biscuit. There's even a snicker from Ramon, in the amulet in my jacket pocket.

"Mom!"

She waves away my embarrassment like it's a pesky fruit fly. "Well, do you?"

"Yes," I push out through a clenched jaw. "And extra

socks and my phone charger, and I'll pray at night, and Dad and Uncle Sammy will be there in case I need anything else."

Mom drags me into a hug. "Good luck."

My face crumples, but she doesn't see it. She smells like banana pancakes, after the huge breakfast she prepared for us before we take off for Las Vegas. She and Auntie Sisi are staying home, thanks to tricky work schedules and limited minivan seating. So this hug could be the last one I give her if I fail to break the curse. Even though she doesn't believe in all this and fought me at every turn, the thought stings, and I squeeze her a little tighter.

"Oh, Freddie, you'll be fine. It's only a couple days."

And I can't even tell her how wrong she might be. A mumbled "yeah" is all I manage.

She squeezes me back.

When I pull away from Mom, my basketball shorts swish around my legs, causing the lucky pennies and rabbit's-foot keychains to clink against each other in my pockets. I pray she doesn't hear them.

I clung to these good luck charms the past few days like my life depended on it. It doesn't even matter if they actually work. They at least make me feel like I'm doing something other than twiddling my thumbs until I get to Ingo.

Waking up to a new notch on the amulet each morning was stressing me out. They're like hands on a ghastly clock, ticking down to my death. I've been extra careful. I've stayed away from anything remotely risky. I even cut my barbecue ribs into small, non-choke-size pieces before scarfing them down last night.

Despite my prayers, Mom's eyes narrow and somehow manage to home in on my shorts pockets. "Wait, what's that noise?"

I kick at the concrete driveway. "What noise?"

The innocent act doesn't work for a second. She juts out a hand, palm up. "Hand them over."

"But—"

"Now."

Grumbling, I empty my pockets and dump the grimy pennies and furry keychains in her hands. Her fingers cage tightly around them.

"You don't need these," she says. "You're going to be the star of the show."

I highly doubt that. "Can I go now?"

With one hand clutching all of my confiscated charms, she uses the free one to ruffle my hair. "Knock 'em dead, Freddie."

If the curse doesn't knock me dead first.

Dad does his ritual body pat for his keys, cell phone, and wallet, then announces, "All right, everyone in."

"We've got a long drive ahead of us," Uncle Sammy

announces from the driver's seat. He punches the hotel address into his GPS phone app, then groans. "Traffic's already bad getting out of the city. It'll take us six hours to get there."

Extra time stuck on the road, on top of an already long drive.

I round the corner of the van and drop my backpack on the seat. To my horror, Dad picks it right back up and hands it to me. "You're in the back row, Freddie."

My stomach gives a warning churn. "But I get carsick in the back row!" And six hours is a lot of time to fight to keep all those pancakes in my stomach.

Dad shakes his head. "With your Apong's hip and Sharlene's ankle, it's too tough for them to make it back there."

I eye the narrow space between the seats. He's right, of course, but that doesn't make the seat assignment any less stomach-gurgle-inducing. I weave my way to the cramped backseat. My knees manage to collide with every possible surface on the way.

I wedge my backpack between the other bags crowding the back row, then slump down until my shins are flush against the back of Sharkey's chair.

With one last wave at Mom and Auntie Sisi, Uncle Sammy puts the minivan into reverse.

That's when I see it again, that shadow right at the edge of my vision, just like before Sharkey's stumble and Apong's fall. I swivel to face it, and I think I see two arms outstretched, like they're ready to push, but focusing on the shadow is like trying to grab a fistful of fog.

"Freddie, do you sense something too?" Ramon asks from the amulet.

His question speeds up the already quickening thump in my chest. Everyone in the minivan is seated and buckled in. No one is getting shoved off their feet this time.

"Yes, but I don't see how—"

The lurch of the minivan and crunch of metal cuts me off.

The wall of luggage avalanches onto me.

"Freddie! Are you all right?" Ramon's see-through hands attempt to pick up a bag that's pinned my shoulder.

"I'm alive," I reply. Alive, but shaken up. I push away the bags and wriggle out of the pinch of the seatbelt. I peek out of the back window and make eye contact with the wide-eyed driver whose blue sedan is scrunched up against our bumper.

Mom, Dad, Uncle Sammy, and Auntie Sisi spring into action. They pull out cell phones, check on the other driver, and help Apong Rosing up for a full once-over to make sure she's okay. None of us seem to be physically hurt, but this fender bender is an earthquake to my confidence.

I can't help the tremor in my voice. "Those spirits are really out to stop us. Even if it kills us," I say once Sharkey and I are alone in the van.

Sharkey angles in her seat to look at me. "It's a good thing they don't know about these new braking features in cars. That car would've hit us a whole lot harder."

Behind the sedan are black tire streaks. The driver really must have slammed a foot on the brakes to avoid us, but it was too late. I gulp.

The door next to Sharkey slides open, and Dad's standing outside, his hands on his hips. "Might as well get up and stretch your legs, you two. We've got to take care of this, and it's probably going to take a while."

Ramon projects himself into a seat once Dad goes back to speak with Uncle Sammy and the other driver. "What is going to take a while? This auto works, does it not?"

Sharkey unbuckles her seatbelt. "Yeah but they have to take pictures and trade car insurance stuff."

"Car insurance? What does this mean?" The frustration in Ramon's voice rings out clear.

My finger traces the twelfth notch on the amulet as I look at him. Ramon said he died thirteen days after angering the spirits by stealing Ingo's amulet. Time is slipping through my fingers like a dodgeball in PE.

"It means we're not going to get to Las Vegas until late tonight." A mush of fear, stomach acid, and pancakes sloshes around in my gut. "It means I have only one more day to break this curse, or I'm dead."

TWENTY-THREE

*E*VERYTHING ABOUT THIS HOTEL SCREAMS "LUCKY."
Spotless marble floors stretch out before me. Chandeliers as wide as a school bus sparkle overhead. In the fountain in the middle of the lobby, crystal-clear water trickles from jugs held by stone mermaids. Even the air smells lucky somehow, scented by tall vases overflowing with fresh flowers (and by all that cash changing hands nearby).

I had a good feeling about this place from the second we checked in last night. I still watched my step on those slippery floors and avoided standing anywhere near those chandeliers and easy-to-tip-over vases, though.

We made it to Las Vegas in one piece, despite the check-engine light glowing bright on Uncle Sammy's dashboard. Once we dumped our bags in the room, Sharkey and I were raring to find Ingo. But Dad didn't think it was a good idea for a couple of twelve-year-olds to go traipsing around Las Vegas alone at night. He didn't think sleepy Apong Rosing was a suitable chaperone either.

This morning, Apong is all energy. So is Sharkey. I, on the other hand, didn't sleep a wink. It's hard to nod off when you're worried about murderous spirits lurking around every corner.

While Uncle Sammy pays the bill for the quick breakfast we scarfed down at one of the casino's restaurants, Dad hangs Apong's purse on the back of her wheelchair.

"How about we do some exploring?" he says. "I hear there's a fountain that does this big show every hour."

He seems so eager to be here that I hate to rip away his excitement. I had a hard enough time hiding my nervousness at breakfast. How would I explain to him that it's not pre-show nerves? That I'm actually worried I may fail and this will be the last time he, Apong, and I have waffles together? I tried to savor what could very well be our final meal and blame the orange juice for the acid gurgling in my stomach.

It's almost nine in the morning on the thirteenth and last day of this curse, and I don't know how far the spirits are willing to let me get today. I can't waste any more time.

"I, uh . . ." I grapple for an excuse. I shoot a look at Sharkey, who's tucking her room key into her backpack.

She slides her headphones down to hang around her

neck, a well-planned lie already on her lips. "Actually, Uncle, the sooner we can get to the practice room, the better. We missed a whole afternoon of practice yesterday, and Freddie could probably use the extra rehearsal time."

I agree, probably too enthusiastically, based on the suspicious micro-tilt of Dad's head.

"While they practice, we can sit at the slot machines," Apong Rosing adds, with a conspiratorial wink at me. Hopefully, for both our sakes, this is the last time I'll need her help. "I have a full coin purse, and I'm feeling lucky." She jingles her yellow floral-print purse in emphasis.

Apong Rosing's demand, the digital sound of coins falling, and a white-haired woman shrieking "I won! I won!" catch Dad's attention. He nods absentmindedly. The pull of the casino is too mesmerizing for him to put up much of an argument. "Okay, then. Let me just figure out what Sammy's doing."

He wanders over to Uncle Sammy, and while they're chatting, Apong Rosing grabs the sleeve of my shirt and tugs me closer.

"Where are you really going?" she whispers.

"Oasis Elder Care."

She squeezes my arm. "Then I will keep your dad on the casino floor and away from those practice rooms as long as I can." A solid offer, given that the spirits will be focused on me.

Apong looks up then at Ramon, who has cast himself next to me.

There's a droop to his shoulders and a sad furrow to his brow. If we succeed, breaking the curse means his spirit will be freed from its amulet jail and he'll be gone—really gone this time. This could be his last moment on Earth with his sister. I realize I wasn't the only one thinking about farewells during breakfast.

"This is goodbye again, isn't it?" Apong Rosing says to him. She worries the wheelchair arm with her short nails.

For a moment, I see them as they were in that family picture at home. Six-year-old Rosita and her older brother, shifting in their stiff formal clothes, unaware of how little time they had left together. I wonder if she had that same look of heartache on her face when she watched him march off to war.

Ramon nods and gives her a small smile. "From what I recall, you never actually said goodbye when I left. You said 'good riddance.'"

Mischief twinkles in her eyes at the memory. "You were such a pest! I still missed you, though."

I snicker to myself. I used to think there was something wrong with us, for not being a family that throws around I-love-yous easily. But we joke and laugh together and ask each other a dozen times if anyone's hungry, and I'm realizing that affection isn't always straightforward announcements like that. It's making sure someone has clean underwear packed for a trip, or taking a few more seconds together even though you're in a hurry, or offering to help a cousin even if it puts you in danger. Part of me regrets not giving my parents some grand goodbye—if today's really going to be my last day alive—but after seeing Ramon and Apong, I think my parents will get the message.

"Don't you worry," Ramon says to his sister. "We will see each other again soon."

Her jaw drops, and she swats at his projection. "What? I've got plenty of years left to live! You're the one disappearing with this curse!" She rolls her eyes at Sharkey and me; we're trying our best not to laugh at Ramon's failed attempt at being sentimental.

Ramon lays a hand on hers as they exchange smiles.

As much as I want to give them a minute longer, I cut in. "We've got to go find Ingo. We don't have a lot of time."

Apong Rosing nods and dabs at the tears that have started to form in her eyes. She smiles one last time at her brother. "Go. Good riddance."

He laughs and vanishes back into the amulet.

Sharkey gives a loud warning cough as our dads approach. She signals for us to start walking.

"Okay, we've gotta run! The first round's at noon," she

calls over her shoulder to our dads and Apong Rosing. "We'll see you in Grand Ballroom A then."

As we drift away from them, I wave at Dad one more time. He flashes me a thumbs-up before turning to Apong.

I shake off the heaviness of the potentially-forever good-bye and focus on the mission ahead. I sneak out my phone to check the time. "That gives us three hours to get to Oasis Elder Care, give Ingo the amulet, and get back here in time to get onstage."

"We're cutting it real close to stage time," Sharkey says.

"Stage time won't even be a problem if I'm dead."

Ramon projects out of the amulet to hover at our side as we pad down the red and gold carpet toward the exit. "How exactly are we getting to this Oasis place?"

Sharkey tugs a wad of cash out of her basketball shorts. "Dad gave me some money for snacks. We can take a taxi there. Did you bring any money, Freddie?"

I blink. I was so focused on that thirteenth notch this morning that I'd only thought to grab my cell phone and the amulet as we left for breakfast. I don't have a room key, and we can't chase our dads down for a copy right now.

Sharkey frowns at my blank expression. "I'll take that as a no." She shoves her money back into her pockets. "Let's hope this gets us there."

TWENTY-FOUR

ONE CAB SITS OUTSIDE IN THE CASINO DRIVEWAY, AND I grin at it like it's a shining golden chariot propelled by unicorns.

"There, one left!" I move in the direction of the yellow sedan.

"Oh no," Sharkey groans. "That family's heading for the cab line too."

I follow her gaze to a whole family in purple T-shirts, practically racing to our cab. We all want that last available car. I pick up my pace. The purple T-shirt father glares at me and whispers to his wife. The family speeds up.

I'm about to break into a sprint when I remember Sharkey behind me. My legs grind to a halt. Sharkey is moving as fast as she can, but it's not a good idea for her to test her healing ankle. There's no way we'd get to the cab before that frighteningly fast family of five. And the cab's not worth the extra jostling to someone who's only injured because of my curse.

"Take your time," I say as the purple T-shirt family loads into the taxi. The young girl in pigtails sticks her tongue out at me.

There isn't another cab in sight. I pull up the map app on my phone as Sharkey catches her breath and stretches her ankle. We'd been shielded from the heat in the minivan and then in the hotel, but I feel the desert sun's growing ruthlessness now. Even though it's only April, the unseasonable heat wave has the temperature burning a good twenty degrees hotter than back at home. I squeeze myself into the tiny sliver of shade from a towering palm tree.

Ramon projects next to me and scans the casino driveway. "How are we supposed to get there now? Do you require my navigation assistance?"

"I can't walk sixteen miles in a hundred-degree heat," I say. I can barely make it through the required one-mile run in PE.

"No giving up," Sharkey says, her hand shielding her squinting eyes from the sun. "Freddie's not getting off the hook on those skate park hangouts with me yet. That bus

—maybe that will get us closer to Henderson." Her gaze fixes on an ad-covered bus idling at the corner.

Maybe it's the fact that the spirits were satisfied with my frustration at the cab, but when I ask the bus driver if this bus will get near the intersection Oasis sits on, she nods.

Sharkey feeds crumpled dollar bills into the fare collector, and I go to snag us some seats.

"No seatbelts?" I eye the multicolored benches, worried.

Sharkey shoulders past me. "Just sit, Freddie."

We collapse into the closest empty seats and let the high-powered air-conditioning evaporate the sweat that's begun beading on our brows. On my map app, I follow our bus's path down East Flamingo Boulevard.

Even though the word *Express* was painted on the side of the bus, it's taking us a lot longer to cover sixteen miles than I thought it would. About twenty minutes into our ride, Sharkey's nodding off, and I'm staring so intently at my map app the image is probably seared into my eyeballs.

I get up to slide a paper bus schedule out of the brochure holder at the front of the bus.

"It says it takes thirty minutes to get to Henderson from our hotel stop, so we're getting close at least. How are we on time?" I ask Sharkey.

She peeks down at her neon green watch. "Two and a half hours until showtime. We should be okay."

And as if the ease of her words summoned a challenge, something dark blurs at the corner of my vision.

I can't help the "oh no" that escapes from my mouth. The paper bus schedule drops out of my hand.

"Freddie . . ." Ramon warns from the amulet. "The spirits. They're coming."

"We have to get off this bus right now!"

Sharkey sits up. "But we're still a couple miles away from—"

"I said now!" I shriek, ignoring the curious looks of the people at the back of the bus. "How do I stop this thing?"

"Pull that cord, little dude," a white man in a shimmering green vest calls to me.

I follow his pointed finger to a metal cord strung over the window. I lunge for it and tug. A *stop requested* tone pings out of the bus speakers.

I'm too late.

A loud pop echoes through the bus. The whole vehicle wobbles. Gasps escape from the bus driver, the people from the back, and even Ramon. Sharkey, eyes wide as the steering wheel, grabs for the metal pole to her right to keep from sliding off the chair completely. My own clawlike grasp on the cord is the only thing that keeps me from splatting onto the dried-soda-stained floor.

"Hold on, folks!" the driver shrieks as the bus wobbles some more.

I tumble back down into my seat, clutching the same pole Sharkey's latched on to.

We let go only when the bus lurches to a stop.

The driver throws the bus into park, opens all the doors, and everyone spills out onto the hot sidewalk outside a grocery store. I help Sharkey hop down the steps and onto the curb. We frown into the suddenly unbearable sun. But I'd take being hot over broken bones and bruises any day.

One look at the bus tells me the curse has caught up to us. The bus's massive back tire is nothing but tattered black rubber.

"Blew out a tire," the driver complains into her walkie-talkie. She bites her lip as whoever is on the other line responds. She turns to the group. "Sorry, folks. This bus is outta commission. The next one's coming in half an hour."

The other riders groan and pluck out their cell phones. I, on the other hand, see nothing but the full set of notches scarring the amulet. Between that and the rocky bus ride, I think I'm going to throw up.

"How far are we from Oasis?" Ramon asks, yanking me out of my thoughts.

I pull up my app. "About a mile. A twenty-minute walk."

"A twenty-minute walk if you don't have a sprained ankle," Sharkey grumbles.

"And if it didn't feel like a thousand degrees outside."

Ramon's eyebrows gather. "Can't you call your father?"

"Do you actually want me dead? Because I guarantee you, if I call my dad, he's either going to kill me for this whole Vegas trip or he's going to take away the amulet and the spirits will do the work by the end of the day."

The three of us let out a sigh in unison. We're too far from all the fancy hotels to catch a cab, and waiting for the next bus would eat up precious minutes we don't have.

The faintest hint of dark creeps at the corner of my vision. "Oh no," I whisper. "The spirits, they're still here."

This grocery store parking lot holds all sorts of Freddie-ending hazards. Drivers on their phones, potholes in the pavement, rusting streetlamps that could teeter over at any second.

"We must find a way to get to Oasis," Ramon says urgently.

"And quickly," Sharkey cuts in, "without the need for bunches of cash we don't have."

The tinny clatter of metal nearby draws my attention to the overflowing corral of shopping carts. The idea forms in my head as a frown spreads across Sharkey's face.

Looking both ways before dashing across the parking lot, I grab a grimy shopping cart abandoned at a nearby planter and wheel it back to the curb.

"Hop in," I tell Sharkey. I'm not about to wait around to see what other catastrophes the spirits are concocting.

She squirms like the shopping cart is even filthier than my room, but she doesn't complain as she climbs in.

I pull up my map app, and Sharkey holds my phone for me.

The app says, "Head east," in its robotic voice, and Ramon instantly points us in the right direction.

"We're twenty minutes away from Oasis. But with this" —I wrap my hands around the cracked orange handlebar — "I bet we can make it in ten. Still, now might be a good time to say a prayer."

Sharkey snorts. "I've been mentally praying the rosary since breakfast."

With a running start and a hard push, I send us zooming down the sidewalk.

TWENTY-FIVE

*U*P UNTIL NOW, THE MOST BEAUTIFUL THING I'VE EVER seen was that super-powerful knockout card peeking out of the Robo-Warrior pack I ripped open. The gold and green foil on the card had shimmered in the light, and I swear angels belted out a chorus from on high.

I actually uttered a low "wow" alone on the floor of my room.

But today, the sight of the Oasis Elder Care beats that a thousand times over.

Here, finally in the Oasis Elder Care lobby, I shove another tiny cone-shaped cup of lemon-infused water in Sharkey's direction. She snatches it out of my hand and empties it as I fill my own for the fifth time. Together, we've downed nearly half of this massive jug of free lemon water. On the salmon-pink couch between potted plants, two red-haired women eye us over their magazines, with that "where are your parents?" look on their pinched faces.

That ten-minute run-walk in this thousand-degree heat wrung Sharkey and me dry. I'm too thirsty to be embarrassed.

Ramon laughs from the climate-controlled safety of his coin. "You two had better hope they have public restrooms."

"Ahem." A pointed cough from the check-in desk draws our attention. An orangey-tanned woman with short hair, sky blue eyes, and floral scrubs raises a blond eyebrow at Sharkey and me. Her name tag reads DELLA. "May I help you children?"

Della spits out the word *children* from her thin lips like it's made of dirt.

I finish chugging my water before approaching. I wipe my sleeve across my mouth, sloppily mopping up the missed drops of lemon water. Della frowns.

"We're here to see Domingo Agustin."

Della clacks her long magenta nails on her keyboard. "And you are?"

I rock back and forth on my sneakers. They squeak against the lobby's polished clay-colored tile. Della's frown deepens.

"Friends. He's expecting us."

She pauses her typing. "Where's your parent or guardian?"

"My dad's on a phone call outside. We're interviewing Mr. Agustin for a school project. He told us to meet him here," Sharkey lies, joining me at the check-in desk. Before I can stop her, she snatches a red candy out of the crystal bowl on the counter. I didn't think it was possible, but somehow Della's frown deepens even more. If we annoy her any further, the sides of her mouth are going to hit the floor.

"Is that right," Della replies in a tone that screams, *I don't believe a word that you're saying.*

"Unbelievable. I had drill sergeants friendlier than her," Ramon mumbles from the amulet.

Sharkey snickers, but I freeze the smile on my face. No need to give Della yet another reason to be suspicious of us.

"Well, children," she says, spitting out the word like it's full of earthworms. "I see a note here in Mr. Agustin's file. Seems he had a rather disturbing phone call last week. And that's on top of the recent elder fraud attempts we've been dealing with. His son has asked that we limit nonfamily contact for the rest of this month, unless Mr. Agustin himself initiates it. His son's probably afraid his dear father is going to get scammed again." Della leans back in her chair, her name tag glinting under the fluorescent overhead lights. "And seeing as how you're only 'friends,' as you say, I'm afraid you're going to have to come back later or get his or his son's written permission."

The hopes I'd built so high begin to topple. "But we came all this way . . ."

Della shakes her head, looking much too happy to have disappointed us. "It says right here on my screen: no visitors outside of family."

"But we are family," Sharkey says, perching her fingers on the countertop between her and Della. "We're his grandkids."

Della glowers down at Sharkey's fingers. "Nice try, kiddo. If you were family, you would have said so. And unless your parent or guardian outside shows me some ID to prove the connection to Mr. Agustin, you'll all just have to come back at the end of the month." She waves her hand at us like she's shooing away gnats and peers behind us. "May I help you?"

An older couple squeezes past, practically shoving Sharkey and me out of the way. Della is much friendlier to them.

Sharkey jerks her head toward the entrance, and I follow her. We park ourselves on a wooden bench sandwiched between two palms.

I bury my head in my hands. No shadows hover at the edge of my vision this time, but I don't need to see the evil spirits to know that this is the worst thing that could've possibly happened.

Ramon, Sharkey, and I trekked all the way to this

unfriendly corner of the desert to be barred from even seeing Ingo.

The thick heat is no match for the realization that turns my blood to ice. I'm never going to break this curse: the spirits have made sure of that.

TWENTY-SIX

ON THE BUSY ROAD OUTSIDE OASIS, CARS ZOOM BY FULL of people with far better luck than I have ever had. Or will have.

I keep my head in my hands, my elbows resting on my thighs. This overwhelming feeling of defeat weighs on my shoulders. I can't bear to meet Sharkey's or Ramon's eyes.

Ever since I reawakened the amulet, I had this single-minded goal: get rid of the family curse. My luck would turn around then. No weird accidents. No stumbles off the stage. No bizarre soccer ball trajectories. Once this amulet was back in Ingo's hands, my life would change for the better. I could try things. I could succeed at things. I might even make some actual not-embarrassed-of-me friends.

And in a matter of moments, Della crushed those dreams.

These past few days have felt like climbing the rope at

school. My muscles burn, but I keep pushing, up and up. If I let go, I'll plummet. I'm almost at the top. But Della is a surprise extra ten feet of rope, and I don't know if I have the energy to keep going, let alone hold on. Now I feel like I'm just waiting for the floor to hit me.

I kick at the desert grit on the pavement. I know I need to figure out what to do next. But it's hard to think straight when all I see are those notches on the amulet.

It isn't until her shoe nudges mine that I finally crane up to look at Sharkey seated next to me.

"So what do we do now?" she asks, her voice quieter than usual. The situation really must be bad if it can shush someone as loud as her.

"Go home, I guess. Well, you will. I'm all out of notches. It's the thirteenth day, and I'm going to . . ." I still don't want to say *die*. My lips won't even form the word.

"We can't let you die. We can't give up." Her voice hitches for a second. "Not when you owe me so much for all of this. We haven't even seen that spy movie yet."

My nerves are too raw for me to laugh. "I know I shouldn't let anything stop me from getting to Ingo, Sharkey. But I have no idea how to reach him."

Ramon projects himself in front of us. He plants his hands on his hips dramatically, like he's imitating a teleserye star. "We're so close. Soldiers, oceans, being trapped in that anting-anting. I went through all of this to be thwarted by that terrible woman." He glares in the direction of the Oasis doors.

"That 'terrible woman' is only going to listen to Ingo's son. Maybe we can try to find him," I say. "What are the chances he'd have a change of heart if I explained this curse stuff to him?"

Sharkey shakes her head. "It took us this long to find Ingo. We don't have time to track down his son, too, not with that amulet countdown. And remember how rude he was? He thought we were scammers. He'd probably call the police or sic Della on us."

Ramon starts to pace back and forth. His despair is contagious. Or maybe we're just batting the same emotion back and forth, making each other miserable in some awful game of Ping-Pong.

"There has to be another way in," I suggest.

We all stare back at the building. Then we frown at the big YOU ARE BEING RECORDED signs with matching security cameras at each door and the cactus patches under each of the windows. I can't think of a worse way to die right now than becoming a human pincushion trying to sneak into an elder care facility.

Sharkey shoves her hands into her pockets, then gasps. "Oh no!" She turns her pockets out, and a pack of spearmint gum and a tube of cherry ChapStick fall out. "Where'd the rest of my cash go?"

I glance below the bench, as if somehow we've both managed to miss a wad of bills. But there's nothing else on the dirt besides our footprints.

She punches the arm of the bench. "It must've fallen out when the bus's tire blew."

"So now we don't even have a way back to the hotel."

My mood sours further. Della's not going to let us pass. Ingo's son isn't going to let us get near his father. We can't even trudge back, tails between our legs, without calling our parents. I might as well start writing my own obituary.

Here lies Freddie: beloved son, decent Robo-Warrior player, mediocre dancer, friend to none.

"We'll find a way, Freddie. We have to," Sharkey says with a pat on my shoulder.

"But look at all that's gone wrong. You actually think we still have a shot at breaking this curse?"

She doesn't even pause. "Of course I do. There's a reason they call me Sharkey. When sharks see what they want, almost nothing can stop them. They're vicious!" She hops to her feet, facing me. "Sharks focus on what they want. They hunt. They sink their teeth right in!" She bares her own teeth and growls.

Ramon taps his lip in thought. "I hate to ruin your speech, but I do not think sharks growl."

A low chuckle escapes me, and some of my gloom goes with it.

Sharkey rolls her eyes. "I know that. But I'm trying to make a point here. Be a shark, Freddie! Be a predator on the hunt! For once in your life."

Ramon shakes his head, bewildered. "I don't understand. Are you suggesting he bite the woman at the front desk?"

Sharkey groans, but I get what she's trying to say. It's like what Ramon and Apong Rosing were saying about being bold and brave. Sharkey's not stuck with a family curse herself, yet she's not willing to give up on me. She really is a shark. And maybe I can be one too.

Her words lift me up a little. There *has* to be a way to get to Ingo and break this curse.

A family speed-walks out of Oasis, the two teenage kids already typing away on their cell phones.

"You know, you could be nicer to your grandmother, maybe actually look up from your screen now and then," the mother says. "We don't see her often."

The teenage girl flips her long purple hair behind her. "What? We were just here last month."

The family continues their arguing all the way to the white sedan baking at the corner of the parking lot.

Sharkey frowns and crosses her arms. "You'd think that the staff here would want their clients to have friendly visitors like us."

I watch the family, still bickering, load into their car. "Right. Something more interesting than the same soap operas and grumpy staff. Apong Rosing practically leapt into the minivan when it was time to drive to Las Vegas."

"Believe me, being trapped in one place for so long grows old quickly," Ramon adds. "Any distraction would be welcome."

My ears perk up at his words: a distraction.

If we create a big, flashy distraction, I might be able to sneak past Della and find Ingo. There's a lot that can go wrong in this plan, especially with evil spirits waiting to pounce, but I'm running out of time.

I tug the amulet out from its place in my shirt, and Ramon pauses his pacing to give me a questioning look. For him, for all the Ruizes, and for myself, I need to give this my best, last shot. I need to do something bold. I need to make my own luck.

I angle to smile at Sharkey.

Even in her frustration, she's tapping the beat of the Wyld Beasts' performance song against her leg. Her fingers freeze when she sees the gears whirring in my head.

"I know that look, Freddie," she says carefully. "What's going on up there? Spill."

I repeat Ramon's words. "Any distraction would be welcome." I stand and brush the desert dust off my pants. "And a distraction we can do."

TWENTY-SEVEN

*T*HE ACOUSTICS IN THE OASIS ELDER CARE LOBBY ARE not bad. The beat from Sharkey's phone booms against the tile floors, the thick gold curtains, the auburn wood of the reception desk. It easily drowns out the boring instrumental music pumped through the speakers overhead.

It takes Della half a second to realize where the noise is coming from. And by then, Sharkey and I have already taken our places in the middle of the lobby.

"Hey, everyone!" I shout. I infuse as much confidence and excitement into my voice as I can. I'm basically channeling Tony the Tiger, selling sugar-frosted cereal like his life depends on it. That's me, but with pants. "Are you ready for the sick stylings of Sharkey and the Fredator?"

The three people waiting on the lobby's white leather

couch glance up from their phones and magazines. A gray-haired Black woman in a wheelchair peeks out of a room ahead.

"Good. People are watching us," Ramon says. He stays put in the amulet, looking out for the spirits. I don't know if there's anything in that coin cell for him to hold on to, but I sure hope he's got something in there to keep him steady for the next few minutes.

A nurse in purple geometric-print scrubs lowers her clipboard to stare at us. Our antics are starting to get attention, but we need more of it if my plan's going to work.

Doubt starts to worm through my head as more eyes land on Sharkey and me. I've never done anything this bold and reckless before. Because soccer player, school band trumpeter, Robo-Warrior ace, dance crew member—I've wanted to be all these things, but this curse kept me from them. Or, to be honest, my fear of the curse kept me from them. Over the years, I've let my fear transform into its own type of monster. It sapped away my confidence to feed itself and grow large enough to cast a shadow on everything around me.

But not anymore. I can't let my monsters and these spirits ruin my life and my family. Plus, I've got a long line of Ruizes before me showing me just what's possible. They didn't let their fear stop them from reaching for something better. They fell, they got back up, and they weren't afraid to try and try again.

I'm done being afraid, too, cursed or not.

I cup my hands around my mouth so everyone can hear me. "I said, are you ready for the fresh, fly moves of Sharkey and the Fredator?" My voice squeaks up at the end, but I'm too nervous to be embarrassed. Besides, planting myself in the middle of a public place for a two-person dance performance is far more embarrassing.

The family checking in at the reception desk swivels around to face us. Della's features curve into a sharp frown. I can almost see steam shooting out of her ears.

She stands up quickly, slamming her palms on the desk. "Excuse me, children. What do you think you're doing?"

"Entertaining these fine folks," Sharkey sings out. She breaks into a crossed-arm, leaned-back, cool-oozing stance. On her face is a smirk with so much attitude it makes me want to toss her my lunch money. Then she starts to move.

Even with the wrap on her ankle, she could dance real and figurative circles around me. She moves her arms like they're made of water: each movement smooth as a wave, breaking at the precise, perfect nanosecond. I'd probably smack myself on the nose or dislocate my own shoulder if I tried to do what she's doing.

"Look at her go, folks!" I yell. "Isn't she amazing?"

The little girl waiting at the reception desk with her family lets out a loud cheer and pumps her fist in the air. Sharkey shoots her a wink without the slightest pause in her performance.

A few more faces pop out of the rooms in the hallway right past the reception desk. But I'm waiting for a particular kind of attention, not just from the residents.

I bounce to the bone-bumping beat and throw my hands up into a clap overhead. Each clap louder than the last, each jump higher.

Sharkey's solo slows to a close. Her cheeks are red with exertion. She flashes a smile at me, and that's my cue: it's my time to shine.

She takes up my clapping rhythm, and I dance a few steps forward, buying myself some space. I start the showcase piece I've practiced for hours. To my surprise, it goes well.

My footwork is smoother than the jerky movements I flung around last week. And I actually stay on beat.

A couple of the residents even start nodding their heads to the music blaring out from Sharkey's phone. A whoop comes from around me somewhere. I think it's Ramon, but I can't risk glancing down and breaking my concentration for a second.

Meanwhile, Della, scowling, is on the phone. With her boss or the police, I don't know. But what I do know is that we're running out of time before some authority comes to stop us. I need to ramp this up.

I wave Sharkey back, and she raises an eyebrow.

"I'm going to try a spin," I call to her.

I doubt she can hear me over the music and the crowd's clapping, but judging by the horror on her face, she can read my lips.

"A spin?" The panic in Ramon's voice is clear. "Do you even know how to do one of those?"

I dance around the space, clearing back some of the spectators who have gathered around. "I watched a video online. What could go wrong?"

And there it is, that shock of shadow. I said the magic words.

"The spirits," Ramon whispers gravely.

The shadow darkens and roils and takes up more of my line of sight now. I can almost make out a figure. The spirits have caught up to me, and they're more than ready to unleash the wrath that's been building for nearly thirteen days.

I crack my knuckles. Like my Robo-Warrior card deal with Dale, I'm going to let the bad luck do its thing. *I'm a Ruiz,* I repeat to myself. *I can be bold. I can make my own destiny. I control it, not the other way around.* (Though I pray I don't kill anyone with this move.)

As smoothly as I can, I slap a palm to the floor and lower myself down. I kick my legs up into the air: a move I've seen on YouTube. I win a few surprised gasps. One's even from Sharkey.

The shadow creeps closer into sight. I slide onto my butt and tense my muscles. I ready myself for this very public attempt at a spin.

"Freddie, watch out!" Ramon warns from the amulet.

A navy-blue-clad hulking form stalks down the hallway. Della, the frown still carved on her face, meets the security guard and points at me. Their brows furrow in unison.

Now all eyes are squarely on me.

The darkness moves to the center of my vision then, and for the first time, I truly see it. I see *him*. The spirits that have been plaguing me have taken form. Not just phantom limbs this time. Like Ramon had warned, this form looks like me. Me, with pale bluish skin, bright white hair, and jet-black eyes. Me, wholly unamused.

This spirit version of me has a snarl on his bloodless lips. He looks dead set on making me suffer.

And I'm counting on it.

"Hold on tight, Ramon," I whisper.

I launch my right leg up, letting the momentum carry me

into my next move. My left leg whips in. I bring my whole body into a tight crunch.

I begin to spin.

The music swirls around me, and someone hoots from the lobby couch. I'm actually doing it—I'm actually spinning. Excitement cracks through me like lightning. For a split second, I catch a glimpse of Sharkey's proud fist pump. My parents used to hound me about trying new things. If they could only see me now!

Then it all goes horribly wrong.

My leg catches on something, and I fear, for a moment, that I've tripped someone's grandmother. But because I purposely provoked the spirits, it ends up being worse than that. I've knocked over a lamp.

Glass shatters across the floor. The spectators scream and leap back. A piece of the hot bulb lands in the dried-up grass of a cactus display. Immediately, tendrils of smoke begin to rise, right before a hint of orange bursts up from a candy wrapper someone discarded in the planter.

I gulp. I set out to cause a distraction, and I succeeded.

I just set Oasis Elder Care on fire.

Della screeches. "Everyone get back!"

The security guard lunges for the red fire extinguisher box on the wall. Someone pulls the fire alarm and the ear-splitting tone shrieks around us.

I shoot a look at Sharkey, and she waves me on. "Go," she mouths. She hops over to the couch and starts ushering the spectators outside. She'll take care of my mess. I owe her one. Or more realistically, if I was keeping count, I owe her a thousand.

"Let's find Ingo," Ramon urges.

I don't need to be told again. I weave past frightened residents and bolt down the hallway.

TWENTY-EIGHT

I **YANK OPEN EVERY DOOR ON MY WAY DOWN THE EMPTY** hallway. I know it's a huge invasion of privacy, but I don't have time to be polite and knock. Not with enraged spirits and a mean-looking security guard on my tail.

My shoes slap against the tile. My legs burn from the intense dance moves I forced on my untrained body. The fire alarm is still blaring, but no one seems to be rushing out of their rooms.

"Ingo?" I call out.

The first door leads to a staff break room, the next few to empty resident rooms. I turn the knob on the next closed door, only to find an older white man hoisting up plaid waist-high pants over—I kid you not—red Elmo boxers. What is it with this curse and underwear?

The man's eyes widen in shock. "Excuse me, young man!"

"I—sorry!" I manage to blurt out before pulling the door shut.

"Perhaps he shopped the same undergarments sale as your mother," Ramon says.

The blood rushes to my face, but now is not the time for embarrassment. I move on to the next door. "You know, you're not really helping."

"If I could physically turn a doorknob and help you search, I would."

The next few doors don't yield anyone matching Ingo's description either. Frustration starts replacing the adrenaline in my veins.

I turn the corner and nearly choke. Another dozen doors lie ahead of me. "Ugh, how big is this place?"

"Where'd that kid go?" The security guard's roar chases me around the corner.

My heart dives into my stomach. That diversion didn't give me as much of a head start as I would've liked.

"Quick, hide!" Ramon says.

I can't exactly wedge myself behind the cactus pots and the grandfather clock in the hallway, so I barrel through the nearest double doors.

Big mistake.

I find myself in the middle of a recreation room. A big-screen television in the corner plays *Wheel of Fortune* reruns to a comfily seated crowd of knitting, gray-haired ladies. Two East Asian men are arguing over a Scrabble board nearby. One man is asleep in an oversize leather recliner, a newspaper crumpled in his lap.

"Pssst."

I swivel my head to find the source of the noise.

An older brown man with white hair smushed down by a black flat cap waves at me. He's seated at a card table with a tan woman with a dyed-black bob, a bald brown man in a maroon sweater vest and gold-rimmed glasses, and a Black man with a thick, Santa-Claus-style beard. The other three are concentrating on the playing cards in their hands. They barely even seem to care that I'm here or that the fire alarm is still wailing away.

I approach them cautiously.

The black-capped man waves faster. "You're hiding from Hector, aren't you? Here."

He kicks his leg at the white tablecloth covering the card table to reveal a dark empty space, bordered by creased-slacks-covered legs on all sides.

His words have the same slow rhythm as Apong Ros-ing's, which makes me feel a little bit better about trusting him. I don't have time to second-guess the offer of help, so

I scurry under, just in time to hear the double doors swing open again.

I tuck my legs close to me, nearly knocking over the plastic bottle labeled FINEST WHISKY the card players had stowed in this hiding place. I peer out from under the hem of the tablecloth.

The security guard is standing by the doors, his hands on his hips like he's a superhero. "I'm looking for a boy. Black hair, green shirt with a pizza on the back. Have you seen him?"

The bearded man to my right huffs. "We're in the middle of a game here, Hector. We haven't seen anyone."

Across the room, a yellow-shawled Latino woman on the couch grunts. "Turn up the television. I can't hear what letter the girl with the glasses chose. Did she buy a vowel?"

Something slaps the table above me. "You've gone and broken my concentration!" the woman playing cards snaps. "I'm going to lose because of you!"

"Don't blame your losing on Hector," the black-capped man says. "You've always been terrible at pusoy dos, Marisol."

Then his legs jerk, as if Marisol's smacked him. I curl myself into a smaller ball to avoid getting kicked by his all-black tennis shoes.

The security guard grimaces. "Shouldn't you all be evac-uating? Come on, everyone. Up. The fire alarm's ringing."

Another one of the women at the couch shushes him. "It's probably Jim trying to smoke in his room again. I'm not rushing out in the heat for that."

The other knitting women mumble in agreement. No one moves.

Hector the security guard takes a few steps further into the room, and I shrink myself more. If everyone evacuates, who knows how long I'll be stuck under this table with my search stalled? It's not like I can blend in with a group of senior citizens as they make for the exit.

"I said up!" Hector bellows. "You know the drill. I can't let you—"

The alarm stops and leaves Hector yelling way too loudly.

"—stay here." Frustrated, Hector rubs the back of his neck. "Della must've tamed that lobby fire. I'll go see if they still need us out of the building. But you'll tell me if you see the kid?"

"Yes, yes," Marisol barks. "Now let us get back to our game, will you?"

Seconds later, I hear the recreation room doors swing open and closed.

I let myself exhale as I uncurl.

"You can come out," the bearded man says with a chuckle.

I crawl out, stand, and wipe my sweaty palms off on my shirt. All four people at the table stare at me.

The man in the sweater vest straightens the cards in his hands and sets them down on the table. "You want to tell us why you're running from Hector? You steal some of that front desk candy?"

The others at the table snicker, like they see this all the time.

My heart slams against my ribs as I try to catch my breath from the chase.

Ramon pssts at me from the amulet. "Freddie, I think that is him!"

"Which one?"

"In the black cap! But he's so . . . old."

I take a second look at the black-capped man, who has now raised an eyebrow at the fact that I appear to be talking to myself. His skin is a dark pecan-brown and so are his eyes. With his broad, flat nose and his accent, I suspect he's Filipino.

"Well?" the black-capped man asks. "What are you doing here, anak?"

I might not have been sure that he was Filipino, but judging by his easy slip into Tagalog, he seems certain that I am.

"I'm—" I swallow to wet my suddenly dry throat. "I'm looking for Domingo Agustin."

The bearded man chuckles again and sets down his cards. "All right, then, time for a break."

Marisol scoots her chair back. "I could use a trip to the little girls' room. Next game in ten?"

They and the sweater-vested man begin to rise, and so does my panic. "Where are you all going?" I reach my arms out as if I could pin them back down in their seats and make them listen to me. "I need to find Domingo Agustin right away. It's a matter of life and death! You're not going to turn me in to Hector, are you?"

"Relax, kid. We're not telling Hector." The bearded man slaps a hand on the black-capped man's shoulder. "We're just giving Ingo here a chance to catch up with his junior fan club, one-on-one."

TWENTY-NINE

*A*LL OF THESE YEARS OF BAD LUCK, THE HUNDREDS OF nights turning over each fresh embarrassment in my head, the mornings spent dreading the next awful unknown. The relief of it all crashes into me like a freight train.

In front of me is Domingo Agustin, the key to the end of this curse.

I'm so completely ready for this to be over that I chuck the amulet straight at him like it's a hot potato.

But this ninety-something-year-old man is not expecting an aerial assault from a strange kid. The amulet smacks him right on the nose and plops into his lap.

Ramon gasps. "Freddie! What in the world are you doing?"

"I—" I blink at him, then at utterly confused Ingo, who is rubbing his sore nose. "I'm breaking the curse."

"This is not a game of tag! You cannot just pelt him with the anting-anting!"

The guilt over what I've done hits me, and I rush over to apologize. Ingo doesn't seem to hear Ramon at all: not a good sign. He's supposed to be able to see Ramon if he believes in curses. Heck, he's the one who cast it in the first place. I exchange a look with Ramon, who seems as worried as I feel.

"Sorry about that," I start to say. Finally remembering my manners—thanks, Apong and Ramon—I grab Ingo's hand. I mano, bowing slightly to press his hand to my forehead as a sign of respect to an elder. Because oh boy, do I need to show that I respect him and am not going to unleash some more surprise coin attacks.

But Ingo's already forgotten about his nose. He lifts the amulet up against the fluorescent overhead light. The sunlight from the window nearby hits the notches, giving the coin an eerie, otherworldly glow for a moment.

"Where did you get this, anak?"

I take one of the newly vacated seats next to him. "I found it in our garage. Do you remember Ramon Ruiz?"

He casts a foggy glance at me. Not a heated reaction like when we called him a week ago.

"How about Rosa Ruiz?"

No hint of recognition flashes across his face.

My chest constricts. At least he's not yelling at me, like he did during our phone call. Then I remember what his son had said: *It isn't a good day for this.*

I've heard that phrase before. I know it.

Ingo has good days and bad days, just like Grandma Nita's neighbor who has Alzheimer's disease. That neighbor has trouble with his memory, and maybe so does Ingo. Maybe he was having one of those bad days when I called. I lobbed so many questions at him all at once: no wonder he got so upset.

Ingo could be the only one who can save me from the spirits bent on killing me off. But first, he has to remember he cursed our family to begin with. That's why he can't sense Ramon. He's forgotten about his best friend, his anting-anting, his curse.

I have to help him remember.

I scoot my chair closer to him. "You're from Santa Maria, right, Mr. Agustin?"

He gives a slow, encouraging nod.

My mind goes to the family tree board from a couple of weeks ago. I zero in on the section just above Apong Rosing's, the two nameplates that I accidentally superglued to my own fingers that late, rainy night.

"Their parents were Jose and Magdalena Ruiz. Jose was

a politician, and Magdalena was famous for her baking. I hear she made a killer brazo de mercedes." I'm ninety-nine percent sure I butcher the pronunciation of that dessert. But something warm flows into me as I speak the names of my great-great-grandparents, as if they too, wherever their spirits may be, are watching. Maybe their hearts ached watching generations of their descendants fall prey to the same curse. Maybe I, not-so-great-at-everything Freddie, am just the kid they were waiting for to break the patterns that held the Ruizes back.

Ingo moves his mouth then like he can taste that brazo de mercedes. Then his eyes widen. "You! A boy called. With a girl, about a project. That was you?"

I nod, trying to gloss over the fact that Sharkey and I lied to him. Between that and the thrown amulet, our friendship is not off to a great start. "I'm Freddie Ruiz, Rosa's great-grandson, so Jose and Magdalena's great-great-grandson. Do you remember Rosa now? And her brother, Ramon?"

I try to keep my voice even and calm after having attacked him with my overeagerness, but I need him to hurry up and remember. Any second, the spirits could find me, and they're not going to be pleased that I used their power against them.

Ingo leans back in his chair and rubs a hand over his chin.

"Yes, yes. I do remember the Ruiz family. The house with the white flowers out front. You know, Rosa always told my parents when I was up to no good."

That sounds like Apong Rosing, all right.

I nearly jump up at the sheer joy that we're finally getting somewhere. I'm about to explain the curse to him when Ramon projects himself at one of the other empty seats at the table.

"Hoy, Ingo, it's me!"

Ingo drops the amulet. It thuds on the table, next to his cards and his glass of water. The glass reflects the shock on his face, the dread on mine, and the empty chair containing the ghost of his long-gone best friend. Ingo follows Ramon's voice to the chair, where Ramon's projection glows brighter than ever.

I was trying to break this whole curse news to Ingo kindly, and here Ramon is, practically bonking him over the head with an anvil.

Ingo leans in to inspect the projection of his friend. He puts out a wary, trembling hand as if he's going to try to touch Ramon's arm, then puts it back down. "Ramon! Is that you? But you . . ." His gaze flies to mine. "Am I dead?"

I shake my head. "No, you're alive, I promise. But Ramon? He's here because he's cursed." I pick up the amulet. "He's been trapped in this since he died."

"But how? My curse was supposed to be for the thief."

"Well, you see, the thief"—Ramon drags a hand through his hair—"is me."

Ingo's eyes narrow, and his cheeks start to turn pink with anger. "You? How could you? You were my best friend!"

Ramon puts his palms together, like he's praying. Or begging. "I shouldn't have stolen it, I know that now. I am so very, very sorry."

Ingo stands so suddenly he knocks his chair over. "Sorry? You're sorry? Do you realize what you did by robbing me of my good luck? My family's rice mill was destroyed! Everything my father and grandfather worked for, gone. It took us years to get back a fraction of what we lost. My father was never the same."

I throw a panicked glance at Ramon. This isn't going how I thought it would at all. Ingo was supposed to rejoice at seeing his friend, forgive us, then I'd be on my merry, uncursed way. Easy peasy.

But from the betrayal on Ingo's face, nothing about this is easy.

Ramon tries again. "Ingo, I know it was wrong. I am truly sorry if it caused you and your family pain. You must forgive me. You must lift this curse."

Ingo slams a wrinkled fist on the table and the playing cards jump. "I don't have to do anything. My family suffered because you robbed me of my good luck. I'm fortunate to have survived the war at all. The way I see it, you deserve what you got. Take your apologies and get out of here."

"No!" The word escapes me so loudly and unexpectedly that even the *Wheel of Fortune* ladies peer over. I lower my voice. "Please, Mr. Agustin. The curse—it affects our whole family, not just Ramon."

Ingo raises a bushy eyebrow. "You too? But you're just a boy. I didn't intend for the curse to hurt you."

"The curse followed my family," Ramon cuts in. "You set evil spirits after us, and now they're trying to kill Freddie."

I pick Ingo's upended chair off the ground and set it right. "Mr. Agustin, I've lived my whole life afraid because of your curse. I don't go anywhere or do anything because I've been hurt too many times. Embarrassed too many times. And being this self-imposed boring means I don't have too many friends. Okay, other than my cousin, who has to hang out with me because, well, she's my cousin."

Ingo sits back down.

I continue. "You should hear how Ramon talks about the good times he shared with you, his best friend. I wish I had something even remotely like that."

They glance at each other then, and the anger starts to drain from Ingo's face. Now he looks just as sad as Ramon.

"If you don't lift this curse, I'm going to . . ." I gulp. "Die. And I won't ever even get the chance to find a friendship like the one you and Ramon had."

Ingo sighs, and his shoulders droop. When he speaks, he sounds tired. "Why did you do it, Ramon? Why did you steal from me?"

Ramon leans forward, planting his elbows on the table as if he could actually touch it. "I was frightened. You remember those days, don't you? We all needed luck."

Ingo nods, and his eyes go distant, as if seeing things far away and long in the past. I don't know what he and my great-granduncle saw during the days of the war. It seems that neither he nor Ramon can forget.

Then it's there, that flicker of darkness at the far corner of the room. The spirits have caught up with me again. My blood goes cold.

I don't have much time. These spirits will kill me off early just to stop me from getting rid of them.

"Mr. Agustin, please," I say. "You must lift the curse. Now."

Ingo shakes his head. When he looks at Ramon, I catch the wet gleam in his eyes. "You should have just asked me to borrow it. I don't even know if I could have lent the good luck to you, but I would have tried if you'd asked." He drags his sleeve against his eyes. He gives me a sad smile. "I will help you. You already seem smarter than your great-grand-uncle, Freddie."

"Believe me, I have a whole list of don't-do-as-Ramon-does tucked away in my head." I gulp. "If I live."

"He's a good kid," Ramon says. The pride in his voice plucks at something in my heart. "Not the best at math, but talented at this Robo-Warrior game where you throw cards."

I consider correcting him, but with the darkness swirling at the edges of my vision, I can't waste a single second.

Ramon must sense the spirits too, because he springs up from his chair. "I pray you forgive me for stealing from you, Ingo. Lift the curse. That's the only way the spirits will leave us all alone, the only way I'll be able to continue on to the afterlife."

Ingo straightens. "Okay. For you, my friend, and for you, Freddie."

"Wait," I blurt out as Ramon's words sink in. When Ingo breaks the curse, the evil spirits will be gone. But so will Ramon. And though I'd hate to admit it out loud, I might actually miss my great-granduncle. Sure, he can be pushy and annoying, but he's family. He's even grown to be a friend, and I'm about to lose him.

And from the pained look on his face, he might miss me too.

"Thank Rosita for her help for me. And tell Sharkey I said goodbye," Ramon says with a nervous smile. "She's the best dancer I've ever met, and you should have seen me back in the day. I can dance almost as well as I sing. Poor you, never having been blessed with a song from me."

I snort, despite the growing sadness pressing down on my chest. "Yeah, poor me. I'll tell Apong and Sharkey. Thank you for helping us. I know it's all your fault and everything, but thanks for helping anyway."

He laughs. "You're welcome. And I owe my apologies to you again too, for bringing this down on your head in the first place. You'll be fine, once the curse is lifted. But remember, that does not mean bad things will never happen again. Sometimes it isn't luck . . ."

"It's life," I finish.

A grandfather clock across the room chimes, and the *Wheel of Fortune* credits begin to roll. It's eleven o'clock, and I have an hour to get back to the ballroom and prep for the Spring Showcase—which I can only do if I'm alive.

Across the room the spirit me forms, as if pulling fragments of shadow and evil from the air. He stares right at me, his face emotionless, but his fists clenched.

I can't draw this out any longer. It's time for goodbye.

"Now, Mr. Agustin. Please."

Ingo adjusts the cap on his head and smooths down his

shirt. "I've never broken a curse before, so I'll do my best." He clears his throat and takes on the overformal tone of a midday TV-show judge. "I, Domingo Agustin, forgive you, Ramon Ruiz, for your transgressions against me. I lift the curse that I placed on you and your family. You are free, my friend."

A bloodcurdling shriek shoots out from the spirit me. It hurls itself toward me, and I scramble up. I stagger back, ready to run, but to where? My muscles tense, and I brace for the worst. We were too late. This spirit is going to kill me after all.

But then it begins to disintegrate like a cloud of smoke. Its fingers go first, evaporating into the air. By the time it reaches me, it is only a pair of black, angry eyes. Then they blink away entirely.

I suck in a breath and look to Ramon to celebrate, but his projection is beginning to thin too.

Smiling, his projection flickers, then softens and fades into nothing. In the amulet, his features vanish. Soon, there's nothing left but those broad outlines I saw when I first came upon the coin in our garage.

He's moved on into the afterlife. He looked happy.

I, on the other hand, feel no different. I guess there's no way to tell if you have bad luck until you test it.

I turn to Ingo. "Thank you."

"My pleasure, anak. And I'm sorry that this hurt your family the way it did. I had no idea that my curse would have such power, that my actions would cause pain even generations later. Is there anything else I can do for you?"

My phone roars with Sharkey's signature text tone. I glance down.

You dead yet? If not, it's almost showtime.

"Actually, Mr. Agustin, you don't happen to have money you can lend me for a cab, do you?"

"Maybe. Though it's been a while since I've been to the bank." Ingo leans over and produces a maroon leather wallet from his pocket. He opens it up and plucks out a crisp twenty-dollar bill. "Looks like you're in luck, my friend."

THIRTY

RUNNING FEELS DIFFERENT WHEN THERE ISN'T AN amulet thumping against my chest. But it's back where it belongs now, in Ingo's hands. Back where it always should have been.

As I fly through the hallways, I begin to feel lighter, as if every step shakes off some of the curse's residue. I clutch the twenty-dollar bill tight. My luck is changing.

Della's on the phone, her back turned to me. She rubs her forehead, and says, "No, no emergency here. A small mishap. Some rotten kids."

Hector is nowhere to be found. Maybe he's still searching one of this place's other massive wings. But no one stops me on my way out the double doors. Lucky me.

Sharkey's sitting out on the curb, her hand shielding her eyes from the sun. Around her mill some of the people who were watching our performance. No one pays attention to either of us as a shiny fire truck, sirens blaring, screeches into the Oasis parking lot.

I jog over to Sharkey, and her eyes go straight to my chest, where the amulet should've been. Then, to my surprise, she nearly knocks the wind out of me with a hug.

I freeze. I haven't actually been hugged by her since we were toddlers. Just weeks ago, she didn't even want to be seen at school with me.

She jerks back. "So, seeing as how you're not in fact dead, are you ready to dance?"

I wave the twenty-dollar bill in the air. "Let's get to this showcase."

I shoot my hand out to hail a cab. Somehow, miles away from the busy streets of Las Vegas or even downtown Henderson, a yellow cab swings around the corner. It rolls to a smooth stop right in front of us.

Sharkey's jaw almost drops. "The curse is completely gone, then?"

I open the car door, and cool air wafts out. "And Ramon too."

"Good. I'm glad he's free," she says, sliding onto the seat. "Maybe now you can actually focus on not ruining the show for us."

I round the car and enter on the other side. I buckle my seatbelt and give the cab driver the hotel address.

The horizon is clear. Not a hint of shadow darkens the traffic-free road ahead. I lean back against the leather seat. "I don't want to scare you, but I don't think my dancing's going to get magically better because I'm uncursed."

Sharkey shrugs. "We'll see. You never know: you might just be the star of the show."

———————

The spotlights overhead shine hot and bright, and the rest of the ballroom is so dark I can barely make out the faces in the first row. A loud voice booms, "Let's welcome to the stage the Wyld Beasts of San Diego!"

I plaster on a toothy smile and dash out onto the stage with the rest of the crew. There's applause as we take our places. I think I even hear a hoot from Dad.

I position myself in the back right of the group, mostly hidden from the audience by a kid half a foot taller than me. As slyly as I can, I double-check the drawstring on my black track pants. The cautious gesture is second nature. I don't want to risk shimmying off these loose pants in the middle of the performance. I've had enough underwear mishaps for a lifetime.

In front of me, Layla peeks over her shoulder. "Break a leg, Freddie! You got this."

I know she's wishing me good luck, but the phrase snags on something in my brain. Barely an hour ago, I would've been terrified that this performance would result in exactly that: a broken leg. My hand absentmindedly goes to the place on my chest where the amulet would've been. Whatever happens now, it's all me.

The crowd quiets.

The Wyld Beasts stay perfectly still, waiting for our cue.

My pulse is its own beat in my ears, and every cell in my body vibrates to it. Nervous doesn't even begin to describe how I feel. I'm fresh off a lifelong family curse, and suddenly I think I'm ready to take on this very public dance performance in front of a bunch of classmates, family, and strangers recording with their phones?

I drag in a deep breath, trying to banish the terror as best I can. There's no backing out now. But even if I could, I'm not sure I'd quit.

After everything I've been through, I'm ready to do something bold, something brave.

I'm ready to make my own luck.

The music starts, and I begin to move.

I'm far from being the star of the show, as both

Sharkey and Mom hinted. I don't dazzle the audience with an impromptu spin or backflip. But I also don't fall on my face, trip any crew members, or vault off the stage headfirst. I don't completely ruin Spring Showcase, and that's what matters.

It isn't about luck. Sometimes it's just life. And with my lifetime of awful coordination and one meager week of practice, a passing performance is all I could've asked for. Still, my smile turns genuine. I'm really doing it. I'm here, on a raised, lit-up stage in front of dozens of people, going full-out.

When the music ends, I feel like I could do it all over again. And maybe I will. Without the cloud of a curse holding me back, nothing can stop me. I can stick with the Wyld Beasts or try out for soccer or become the best ever Robo-Warrior player. There are no supernatural obstacles anymore, no excuses. I feel like I can take on the world. But maybe I'll focus on seventh grade first.

Sharkey high-fives me as the crew jogs off the stage. She doesn't even seem the least bit embarrassed to be seen with me. I'd say she might even be a little proud, but she'd probably punch me in the arm if I ever asked her about it.

"Hey, good job out there."

I swivel to find the source of the voice. Dale, who, for once, is actually looking at me with a tiny bit of respect.

"Thanks. And thanks for giving me a chance."

He shrugs before high-fiving a couple more crew members jogging past him. He angles back to me. "Weird question, but you didn't bring your Robo-Warrior cards, did you? I'm having a few people over in my suite for a mini-tournament after lunch. If you're up for it."

I scan his face for any sort of mockery, but he's completely sincere. And of course I brought my Robo-Warrior cards. "Count me in."

As the crew breaks off, Sharkey and I make our way to Dad and Uncle Sammy, still seated in the third row. Dad was streaming the whole performance on his phone. Earlier, as Sharkey and I sprinted into the ballroom, out of breath from our dash from the cab, Dad assured me that Mom, Auntie Sisi, Uncle Ritchie, and even Grandpa Carlo and his third wife would be watching. I appreciate the sentiment, but for all our sakes, I hope they weren't.

Apong Rosing says I did splendidly. I'm fairly certain she napped through most of it.

Wyld Beasts stroll out of that ballroom with our heads high, our participation medals swinging from our necks. As a reward, Dale's father treats us to the hotel buffet, as long as we stay in our Eastside Pizza gear. That means all the ice cream and multicolored Jell-O topped with little tufts of whipped cream I can eat. I'm about to head straight to the dessert section when Apong Rosing seizes my arm.

"Freddie!" she whispers like she has a secret. "I won two hundred dollars at the slot machines!"

"That's great!" I smile at the confirmation that the evil spirits left her alone too.

"So no more curse? My brother is free?"

I nod, and her mouth curves into a warm smile. She makes the sign of the cross, then squeezes my arm. She digs her free hand into her purse. "That means you'll need a new anting-anting, then." She plucks out one of those souvenir pressed pennies, which she must have gotten from the gift shop. "I have a chapel schedule in here somewhere and—"

"No!" I scream, and Apong nearly drops the penny in surprise. I've had my fill of anting-anting and evil spirits for now. I'd much rather spend my time and energy on that unlimited ice cream and Jell-O. I pat her hand. "I mean, I'll be fine without one. Thanks, though."

She slips it back into her purse. "I'll hold on to it for you anyway. You see how powerful this magic is. You never know when you'll need it."

I don't plan on ever relying on another good luck charm again. No four-leaf clovers, rabbit's feet, lucky pennies, nothing.

I help her to the salad bar, then stack a red plastic tray

up with a dangerous number of small, breakable plates of sugar. I scoot into a booth next to Sharkey, who has already made plans for the both of us to attend two movies, a laser tag birthday, and a ramen fest with her friends. Across from us, Uncle Sammy grumbles to himself.

I smile and dig into my first bowl of ice cream. I'm not even going to worry about knocking my drink onto someone's lap, sneezing into the chocolate fountain, or being the only one to get food poisoning today.

From now on, good or bad, my luck is what I make it.

ACKNOWLEDGMENTS

First off, thank you, reader, for joining Freddie and me on this adventure. Getting to this wondrous point at which you're holding a copy of my words in your hands was a long road, but I kept at it, with the help of so many wonderful, dedicated people. This was me, being bold and brave like Freddie, except I had the fortune of having dozens of Sharkeys.

To Natalie Lakosil, my agent, the perfect blend of fierce and friendly—thank you for believing in this story and for being such an amazing champion of my work. Working with you and the whole Bradford Literary team has been a dream.

To Amy Cloud, my phenomenal editor—I am so grateful for your sharp eye and kind words. You challenged me to dig into the heart of the story and inspired me to make Freddie's life worse (but in the best way).

Thank you to the incredible team at Clarion: Celeste Knudsen, Mary Magrisso, Susan Bishansky, Erika West, Zoe Del Mar, and Sammy Brown. Your thoughtfulness in the details wowed me, and I knew this book was in the best hands with you all every step of the way.

To Alane Grace—thank you for bringing Freddie and Sharkey to life on this beautiful cover.

To my writing group, the Guillotine Queens: Rae Castor, Alyssa Colman, Kat Enright, Sam Farkas, Jenn Gruenke, Jessica James, Kalyn Josephson, Ashley Northrup, and Brittney Singleton. I couldn't have done this without your friendship, guidance, and laughter.

A huge thank-you to Alechia Dow, for everything from your boundless generosity, to your spot-on feedback, to the deliciousness you send to our doorstep. To Pamela Delupio —I'm thankful to have such a strong Pinay writer in my corner. To Delara Adams—it means so much to me that I could always count on your support over the years. And thank you to Akemi Dawn Bowman for your warmth, encouragement, and insight.

To Kate Heceta and Megan Ordona: you brought Freddie and his world into closer alignment with ours, and I can't thank you enough.

To my FALSD and NFALA families and my fellow Pinay Powerhouses: Thank you for showing me every day just how bold and brave Filipino Americans can be.

To Traci Adair, Jennifer Franz, Brittani Miller, and Rossini Yen. I am so fortunate to have you all in my life. Thank you for never letting me take myself too seriously. A toast!

My never-ending thanks to my family: Mom, Dad, Reggie, Grandma L, Grandma D, the Aspirases, the Baduas, the Reddys. You always encouraged my reading and storytelling, whether sharing your own tales, driving me to the library or to a faraway place for book research, or packing me days' worth of leftovers so I could spend those extra moments writing. Every good thing in this story can be traced back to you. You make my life magical.

Ruby, you are my heart. I'll try my best not to do anything to bring a family curse down on all of us.

And to my husband, Rahul, my loudest cheerleader and the one who helped me brainstorm all the awful stuff that happens to Freddie. Thank you for pushing me, for moving toddler and earth so I could write, and for ordering champagne or cookies for every little celebration. Life with you is proof of my good luck.